Just My Luck

JUST MY LUCK

JENNIFER HONEYBOURN

Swoon READS

New York

A Swoon Reads Book

An imprint of Feiwel and Friends and Macmillan Publishing Group, LLC
120 Broadway, New York, NY 10271

Our books may be purchased in bulk for promotional, educational, or
business use. Please contact your local bookseller or the Macmillan Corporate
and Premium Sales Department at (800) 221-7945 ext. 5442 or by email at
MacmillanSpecialMarkets@macmillan.com.

Library of Congress Control Number: 2018955603
ISBN 978-1-250-19465-7 (hardcover) / ISBN 978-1-250-19466-4 (ebook)

Book design by Liz Dresner

First edition, 2019

10 9 8 7 6 5 4 3 2 1

swoonreads.com

For my mom

One

People leave a lot of really strange things behind at hotels. In the five months I've worked at the Grand Palms Maui, I've come across some truly weird items—a rubber gorilla mask, a notebook with nothing but *carpe diem* written over and over in tiny block letters, a pair of dentures floating in a glass of water.

And now, a cat.

"Here kitty, kitty." I'm down on my hands and knees, trying to coax the poor thing out from underneath the bed. One of the housekeepers heard meowing when she was cleaning the room, and for some reason my mom decided I was the best person to deal with the situation.

The door to the suite opens. I know it's one of the

other staff, probably Leo, coming to check on me, because this is taking way longer than my mom thinks it should.

"Howzit, Marty. Any luck?" Leo asks.

Luck. That's not something I have much of these days.

I shake my head. "It hasn't moved." All I can see are two wide green eyes staring at me through the darkness.

"Maybe this will help." Leo's knees pop as he kneels down beside me. He holds out an open tin of tuna, and the cat immediately comes out from beneath the bed. She's small, with the same pale gray hair as Leo, and she's wearing a pink rhinestone collar.

"Hello, sweetheart," he says, gently stroking the cat's back as she dives into the food. "Who could leave you behind?"

"Karl and Dana Hudson, that's who," I reply, silently cursing them. "They were the last guests in this room. They checked out this morning."

Leo shakes his head. "I guess there's no point trying to track them down, then. They're probably already on a flight to the mainland."

Maui has a lot of feral cats—seriously, they're everywhere—so it's not exactly a mystery how this cat ended up here. My guess is that this couple decided to "adopt" her during their luxury vacation, thinking they were doing her a favor. And now that they've returned to reality, they've left her behind for someone else to deal with.

Leo sighs and turns to look at me. He catches sight of my face, and his eyes widen. I scowl at him as his lips pinch together, like he's trying really hard to hold in a laugh.

"It's not funny," I snap. I've lived on Maui my entire life; I *always* wear sunscreen. But I clearly didn't apply enough to my face yesterday, because I got a wicked sunburn. Which would be bad enough, but I was wearing sunglasses, so while the rest of my face is the color of raw beef, the skin around my eyes wasn't touched. I look like a raccoon.

Maybe I'd be able to laugh about it too, if this were the only crappy thing that had happened to me lately. But it's just one more thing in a long, long list of things that have gone very wrong for me over the past several months.

A few examples: my computer crashed and wiped out an essay I'd spent a week working on, the morning it was due; I dropped my phone and cracked the screen, and two days after I had it repaired—using the money I was saving for a new laptop—I dropped it again; I was knocked off my surfboard in front of this creepy guy Hunter, and when I came up for air, the top half of my bikini was missing; and I caught my prom date making out with another girl in the back of our limo.

The cat finishes the tuna. Before she can dart back under the bed, Leo scoops her up, cradling her in his arms like a baby. His navy Hawaiian-print shirt is immediately covered in cat hair. Management makes him wear it, along with stiff khaki pants, even though he's the hotel handyman. Khakis aren't the most practical choice when you're unclogging toilets or fixing a broken air conditioner, but Leo doesn't complain. Leo never complains.

"So now what?" he says.

"Now I take her downstairs, I guess." I stand up and smooth out my skirt, which is more habit than necessity—I'm stuck in the same stiff khaki material as Leo, and it never wrinkles. God forbid our guests lay eyes on someone in a wrinkled uniform.

"Your mom isn't going to be too happy to have a cat in housekeeping."

I frown. He's right about that, but I don't know what else to do with her. "She sent me up here. She's going to have to deal."

Leo rubs underneath the cat's chin and her eyes drift closed. She starts to purr. "I'd take her home, but Beth would kill me. She made me promise not bring home any more strays." His voice raises an octave as he says, "You should have a name."

"Don't get too attached. She's probably just going to the shelter." I feel mean saying this in front of the cat, but it's either the shelter or back out on the street.

If Nalani were here, she'd tell me to take the cat home. It certainly wouldn't be the first time I took something from a guest's room. But I know better than to ask my mom if I can keep her cat. She's not exactly Team Marty right now.

"She looks like a Libby," Leo says.

"If you say so." I straighten the bed's immaculate white duvet and glance around to make sure everything is perfect for whoever is checking in next. The people who can afford to stay in the Grand Palms are rich—not just regular rich, but incredibly, unbelievably rich—and they have super-high standards. Although the room is simple—white and airy, like being inside a cloud—everything in here easily costs more than my family makes in a year.

The room still smells like tuna, but hopefully no one will notice. I pick up the empty tin, and Leo and I leave the room. He follows me down the hall, still cooing to the cat. The carpet is so thick, I can't hear our footsteps. When we reach the elevator, he sighs and passes Libby to me before punching the call button.

"Don't just dump her, okay, Marty?" he says.

I nod, but I'm not sure why he thinks I'll have any say in the matter. He'd be better off talking to my mom himself, but I think he's scared of her. Most people are. My mom is the floor supervisor, but from the way she acts, you'd think she runs the entire hotel.

Leo pats the cat one more time, then ambles off down the hall. Libby squirms in my arms like she wants to run after him, and I tighten my grip. The last thing I need is for her to jump out of my arms and take off. I've already wasted too much time trying to catch her.

The elevator dings and the mirrored doors slide open. I stand back as two guys around my age step out.

I flinch. Great. Guests my age are the worst. There's nothing more awkward than having to serve someone who could be sitting behind you in history class. Most of the time we ignore each other—only for different reasons: me, because I'm quietly dying inside; them, because they don't really see me. After all, I'm just the help.

"We need to talk to the locals," the guy with a messy black pompadour says to his friend, a scrawny kid with closely cropped dark hair. "They'll know where the best waves are."

Surfers. Well, wannabe surfers. I see this a lot. Rich kids who come to Hawaii with the idea that they can conquer our waves. They won't get very far talking to any of the locals. We're friendly, sure, but there's a definite line between the places we recommend to tourists and what we save for ourselves.

Libby starts to wriggle again and lets out a sorrowful meow. The black-haired guy's eyes flick to her and then to me. He's good-looking, in an early Elvis, rockabilly kind of way. Skyscraper tall with thick eyebrows and full lips and ears that stick out slightly. Exactly my type. And so, when he smiles at me, a jolt goes all the way through me, right to my toes. And if my face wasn't already burned, there's no way he'd miss me blushing.

Oh my god. My face! He isn't smiling at me; he's smiling at my ridiculous sunburn!

I duck my head, anger and humiliation coursing through me. I'm in such a hurry to get away from them, I don't notice the elevator doors have already started to close until I bump right into them. Libby digs her claws into my arm and I let out a scream.

"Are you okay?" the guy calls, but I pretend not to hear him. The doors have slid back open and I quickly escape inside the elevator. Mercifully, it's empty and the doors slide shut again before he can check on me.

My heart is pounding. *It's fine. This is a big hotel*, I reassure myself. *I probably won't ever see them again.*

But given the way my luck has been lately, I know the odds of not running into them again are not in my favor.

I sag against the back wall of the elevator and close my eyes. How much worse can this day get?

Two

haven't been down to the housekeeping department since I was reassigned to the front desk last month. After my mom caught me sneaking out, she said that if I liked being awake in the middle of the night so much, I might as well do it at the hotel.

She couldn't have come up with a worse punishment. Not only do I have to work vampire hours the entire summer, putting a serious crimp in my social life, but Nalani is mad that I've been "promoted," while she's still stuck cleaning rooms. It's put a real strain on our friendship. I get why she's upset—she's been at the hotel a lot longer than I have. I've tried explaining to her that working the front desk is not nearly as much fun as working with her—for one thing, all the other staff are at least ten years older than I am, and, with the exception of Benjie, most of them have lost their sense of humor somewhere along the way—but she says it's still better than cleaning toilets. And honestly, it's hard to argue that point.

Nalani usually works the day shift, so I'm surprised to see her down here with the other night crew, haphazardly stuffing towels into her housekeeping cart. The huge concrete room is a warehouse of housekeeping supplies—cleaning products, plumbing tools, extra pillows and bed linens—all stacked neatly on tall metal shelves.

She glances up as I walk toward her. Her eyes narrow as she takes in my weird sunburn, the blood running down my arm, the cat desperately squirming to get away from me.

"I have so many questions," she says.

"I don't know where to start," I reply.

Nalani lifts Libby out of my arms and the cat immediately settles down.

"Someone left her behind," I say, grabbing the first-aid kit from one of the metal shelves. I flip it open and take out an antiseptic wipe and a Band-Aid.

She scowls. "God, I hate people."

"How come you're here so late?" I ask, wincing as I gently dab at the scratch with the wipe. Being here at night means my mom is trusting Nalani with turn-down service again—something I never thought would happen after she was caught eating the chocolate-covered macadamia nuts she was supposed to be leaving on the guests' pillows.

I've never helped myself to the macadamia nuts, but I have taken things that don't belong to me. When I was cleaning rooms, I would sometimes take little things I didn't think anyone would miss—things most people would assume they'd just misplaced. Stupid stuff, like a cheap pair of sunglasses or a travel candle. I never took from anyone who didn't deserve it, but still, it was wrong and I feel bad about it.

Nalani shrugs. "Andrea quit, so I'm picking up some of her shifts. We need the extra money. Our trip is coming up fast. Can you believe we'll be leaving in less than two months?"

I swallow and concentrate on cleaning my scratch so I don't have to look at her. Taking a gap year and traveling after we graduated has been the plan since junior year. But so much has changed in my life recently, I just need to stand still for a minute.

If our friendship weren't on such fragile ground, I would have told Nalani months ago that I'm not going with her. But I'm not sure we can survive that bomb-shell and so, like a coward, I keep pretending I'm still on board. I feel super guilty about lying to her. I know I'm not making the situation any better by not telling her, but I don't know how to break the news.

"Are you off this weekend?" Nalani says as I stick the Band-Aid on top of my scratch. She hands Libby back to me and tucks a strand of her short dyed-blond hair behind her ears. "I'm having a party in Kaanapali. Remember the house with the huge pool?"

Nalani's stepdad works for a company that rents luxury houses all over Hawaii. He travels around the islands a lot and her mom usually goes with him. Sometimes they're away at the same time one of the houses on Maui is empty, and since Nalani knows where they keep the keys, we usually take advantage and hang out in these crazy expensive places.

"Is Kahale going?" I know I shouldn't care if he's there—he's the one who acted like a jerk, after all. I haven't talked to him since prom night, when I caught him with his hand down the front of Grace Hamasaki's dress.

Nalani rolls her eyes. "I didn't invite him. Although maybe I should. You could confront him and be done with it."

"I am done with it." But we both know that's not true. I know it bothers Nalani that I avoid confrontation, but honestly, I want to forget the entire night even happened. Just talking about Kahale is making my palms sweat. I only need to steer clear of him for two more months, until he leaves for college somewhere in the Pacific Northwest.

Libby starts to wriggle around again. "I'd better get her in there," I say.

"Saturday. Don't forget," she calls as I walk toward my mom's office.

It's almost eleven o'clock at night—long past the time when my mom should have left for the day—but she's still here, frowning at her laptop. The fluorescent lighting is bright and unforgiving, and it highlights the dark purple bags under her eyes. Two deep wrinkles are engraved on either side of her mouth, the result of all the frowning she's done over the past six months, ever since my dad left. All of her stress and unhappiness is showing up on her face.

"When I said fix the situation, I didn't mean bring it down here," she says without looking away from the screen.

"I didn't know what else to do with her." I can't just stick Libby outside—the hotel is constantly trying to get rid of the stray cats; no one would appreciate me adding another one.

My mom sighs heavily, a sound I've become so used to hearing, I barely register it.

I'd like to tell her to go home, that we can do without the money she makes working overtime, but I know she'll just snap at me. Money isn't the only reason she works so much. She doesn't like being at home. We're still living in the house I grew up in, the one she and my dad bought together when they were first married. He may have moved to O'ahu, but there are still reminders of him everywhere in that house.

"Leave it down here until your shift is over, then take it to the shelter," she says, rubbing her eyes.

Although I knew this was probably what she was going to say, I feel bad for Libby. I don't want to think about what could happen if no one adopts her. It's not her fault she's in this situation.

"What if we—"

My mom's already shaking her head. "Marty. Don't even ask."

I purse my lips. Once upon a time, she would have let me keep the cat. In fact, keeping her probably would have been her idea. But now it's just one more thing she'd have to deal with. One more thing on her already overloaded plate.

And this is why I can't leave Maui.

My older brother, Ansel, is already halfway out the door, and if I go too, I don't think my mom will ever snap out of this funk. Our family is already fractured, but if my brother and I both leave, we'll officially be broken. Someone has to stay behind to make sure that doesn't happen.

"Fine. I'll ask around and see if any of the staff will take her," I say. I set Libby down on the floor then pull the office door shut behind me.

I keep hoping that time will give my mom back to me. But with every day that goes by, I'm less and less sure that she'll return.

Three

"H ey, any chance you want to adopt a cat?" I ask Benjie an hour later. It's past midnight and the front desk is quiet. This is the worst time to be at work, because there's nothing to do, and yet there's still a million hours before my shift ends.

"Zero chance. Leo already asked me," Benjie says. "But cheer up! I know how we can pay those heinous people back for dumping her on us." He taps something into his computer, then swivels the monitor so I can see the screen.

I wrinkle my nose. "You want to send them a glitter bomb?"

"It's the perfect revenge," he says. "They open the envelope and *pow*"—he mimics an explosion with his fingers—"glitter everywhere. They'll be vacuuming it up for weeks!"

"Um, maybe not." The Hudsons are the worst, but sending them a glitter bomb isn't going to help me find a home for Libby.

Benjie's lower lip puffs out. "You're no fun," he says. "Now, I could stand here and try to convince you, but it's been an hour since my last break. I need to eat something or I will faint. You'll be fine on your own?"

I nod. The Grand Palms is in Wailea, an area on the south side of the island that shuts down ridiculously early. Aside from the occasional late check-in or guest complaint, at this time of night it's usually just Benjie and me, jacking around.

When he leaves in search of a snack, I pull out my phone. We're not supposed to use them on duty, but if no one's here to catch me, then does it even really matter? I haven't had it fixed since I dropped it again last month, and the screen is webbed. I'm scrolling through Instagram, trying to talk myself out of checking Kahale's feed, when out of the corner of my eye, I notice someone approaching the front desk. I quickly tuck my phone back into my pocket. I glance up and my breath catches. It's the hot guy I saw in the hall earlier, only this time all he's wearing is a towel.

And ohmygod, his body is *incredible*. He's like a

Greek statue come to life, his chest as hard and polished as cut stone. His dark hair is wet, slicked back from his face. My own face is prickling underneath my sunburn, but he doesn't seem the least bit embarrassed, even though he's the one standing half-naked in front of a complete stranger. His friend is behind him, also wearing only a towel, and dripping water all over the bamboo floor.

"Hey," Hot Guy says, his eyes dropping to the brass name badge pinned on the pocket of my Hawaiian shirt. "Marty. Can you help us? We forgot our room key."

My shoulders stiffen as I remember that, just over an hour ago, this boy laughed at my sunburn. Okay, maybe he didn't laugh, exactly, but he did smile at me and I'm pretty sure it was only because I look like I'm wearing a bandit mask.

Unfortunately, my face hasn't changed since then. It's not easy to pretend that this doesn't bother me, but I have to be polite—it's kind of a job requirement—so I say, "What's your room number?" I sound calm and professional, so there's no way he could pick up on my inner rage.

"7010."

I type the number into my computer.

"The room is registered to my dad, Richard Foster," he adds. "He booked the room for my brother and me."

His dad didn't just book a room—he booked the King Lunalilo Suite. The Fosters are clearly in the top 1 percent, because they're staying here for the entire summer.

God, life is so unfair. Hot Guy gets to live in the lap of luxury, experiencing things that the rest of us could never hope to, even if we lived ten lifetimes. And he didn't even do anything to earn it—he just happened to be born into money.

"What's your name?"

"Will," he says.

Sure enough, there's a note on the file about Richard's two sons—Will and Hayes.

"Do you have ID?" I ask.

Will glances down at his near-nakedness. "Not on me," he says. "I didn't think this through, obviously."

Right.

Hotel policy is not to let someone into a room without proper ID, but I'm pretty sure that he's telling the truth, so I bend the rules and program a key card.

"You know, the pool actually closed hours ago," I say. This time I hear the edge in my voice, and Will must too, because his eyes skip guiltily away from me. He drums his fingers on the counter, and I notice his fingernails are chewed almost all the way down.

"Yeah, sorry about that. We were quiet. Although not quiet enough, I guess. The security guard just kicked us out," he says. "Listen, are you okay? You looked like you ran into those doors pretty hard earlier."

"Oh. Yeah. I'm fine," I reply. "I just wasn't watching where I was going."

His concern knocks me off-balance a bit. He seems genuinely interested in making sure I'm all right. I guess there's a small chance I was wrong about him and he wasn't actually making fun of me earlier. A very small chance.

All of this is going through my head as I hand him the key card. Our fingers brush and my body starts to buzz. A slow smile spreads across his face, like he knows exactly what I'm feeling, because he's feeling it, too.

It's been a while since I buzzed like that and I don't know what to do, so I yank my hand back and take a small step away from the desk. We're staring at each other, eyes locked, when the other guy—who must be Hayes, his brother—marches up to the desk, a striped beach towel wrapped around his shoulders like a cape.

"Okay, you've got the key. Why are you still standing here?" he says to Will, without acknowledging me. "I'm freezing my ass off."

Will's smile tightens. "Right," he says, but his

brother has already stormed off, heading through the lobby, leaving behind wet footprints on the marble.

"I guess I'd better get going," Will says. "Sorry for getting water all over the floor. I'll see you around, Marty."

He walks away just as Benjie reappears, carrying a plate of muffins.

"Let me guess, they broke into the pool and forgot their key," he says, as Will and Hayes disappear into the elevator.

I nod.

"The tall one is cute."

I pick up a stapler, even though I have nothing to staple. "I didn't notice."

Benjie scoffs. "When have you not noticed cute?"

I frown. He's right—every hot guy who crosses our path is usually up for immediate discussion. I don't know why I'm being weird about Will.

That's a lie. I do know why—whatever it was that just passed between Will and me, it's something I haven't felt since Kahale. And look how that turned out. I don't want Benjie to pick up on this, because he will never let it go.

He sets the muffins in front of me. "You like him."

Okay, so obviously I'm not doing a very good job of hiding my feelings.

"I don't even know him," I reply.

"The beginning is the best part of a relationship." Benjie sighs. "I remember those days."

"Those days were not that long ago," I remind him. He's only been with Aaron, one of the hotel's sous chefs, for a couple of months. "And calm yourself. The last thing I'm interested in is a relationship."

"Fine—fling, dalliance, summer romance. Call it what you want," he says. "I call it love."

I snort. "I talked to him for ten seconds." And, okay, it was a pretty meaningful ten seconds, but still. Love is the furthest thing from what that was.

I grab one of the chocolate chip muffins—one of the benefits of working with someone well connected with the kitchen—and take a large bite. I cry out as something crunches horribly in my mouth and an excruciating pain shoots through my gums.

Benjie wrinkles his nose as I spit the muffin out into my hand.

"I think I just chipped my tooth."

"I don't think that's even possible," he says. "Muffins are practically pre-chewed. There's nothing to chip your tooth on."

But he moves a bit closer to me and peers into my mouth. "Oh my god!" he cries. "Half of your front tooth is missing!"

I groan and run my tongue over the jaggedy edge of what's left of my tooth. "Great."

"Maybe they can reattach it or something."

"It's not like a finger," I say, but I dig the shard out of the spit-out remains of the muffin, just in case. My hands are shaking as I drop the shard of tooth into my pocket.

I take a deep breath to try to calm my nerves. My luck seems to be getting worse with each passing day, and it's starting to get to me. I've done everything I could think of to try to flip my karma—no sneaking out, no talking back to my mom (well, mostly), no taking things that don't belong to me. I've picked up every penny I've come across on the street. I feng shui'd our entire house. I've hung horseshoes above my door, bought a rabbit's foot—a faux one, but still. I even considered getting a four-leaf-clover tattoo, until I realized my mom would kill me dead, so I settled for a necklace with a charm of the lucky symbol instead.

I've been a model citizen for an entire month. Nothing has worked. My luck still sucks.

And I have no idea how to fix it.

Four

So it turns out that breaking your tooth is not a good enough reason to leave work early—at least not according to Marielle, our night manager. She points out that the dentist office won't be open for hours anyway, and since the pain has subsided— thanks to a few Tylenol—I should be able to hang on for a few more hours. She's usually a stickler for presenting a professional appearance, but unfortunately for me, it's the middle of the night and she figures I won't be interacting with many guests.

I swear Marielle's out to get me. She was not happy when my mom had me moved to the front desk— apparently she's not a fan of nepotism—and I feel like she's just waiting for me to slip up so she can fire me.

After my shift finally ends, I change into my slippers. I hate the ugly, low-heeled black patent leather shoes that are part of the hotel uniform, so I always take them off the first chance I get. I head down to my mom's office and load Libby into a black cat carrier that Leo left for her, along with a Tupperware container of cat food. I know I should take Libby to the shelter, like my mom asked me to, but one look at her sweet little face and I know I can't do it.

Benjie is waiting for me so we can walk out together. The hotel makes us park our cars a few blocks from the hotel, in a sandy lot next to a construction site. It's not a sketchy area, exactly, but I don't like to walk out there alone before the sun has come up. He's changed out of his uniform and into a white tracksuit. His unruly black curls are tucked underneath a trucker hat.

"How much do you think it's going to cost to have my tooth fixed?" I ask him as we head down the sidewalk. I'm worried, because we don't have dental insurance. And we don't have a whole lot of extra money, especially now that my dad's gone.

Benjie shrugs. "Whatever it costs, it's worth it—it's not like you can go around with half a front tooth."

I sigh.

An older woman out for an early-morning stroll is

coming toward us, walking a huge brown dog. Libby must sense the dog, because she shifts nervously in her carrying case. The dog clearly picks up on her, too, because it starts to bark and strain at its leash. I'm afraid of dogs—especially loud, barky ones that look like they could swallow me whole—so I'm relieved when the woman manages to wrestle control of it. My heart pounds as she crosses to the other side of the street.

"Okay, that was seriously—"

"Marty," Benjie interrupts. "Watch where you're—"

Something makes an awful squish underneath my rubber slippers.

"Walking," he finishes.

My stomach heaves. Even without looking down, there's no mistaking what I just stepped in. The smell wafts up toward me and I gag. "Ew! Ewwwwwww! Oh my god!"

Benjie whips around. "You shouldn't own a dog if you can't clean up after it!" he yells at the woman's retreating back.

I can't even scrape the dog crap off—it's embedded in the bottom of my slipper. I angrily kick off my shoe, tears stinging my eyes. I know this isn't something I should be crying over, but it's the end of a very long, very bad night and I can't hold it in any longer.

I'm sniffling as I set Libby on the ground. Benjie hands me the Whole Foods tote he uses for a lunch bag. I bend down and gingerly pick up my slipper by its yellow rubber strap. I throw it inside the bag, then bend down to inspect my foot.

There's dog poop on my big toe.

Dog. Poop. On. My. Big. Toe.

I shudder, so grossed out that I can't even talk.

Benjie wrinkles his nose. "Boy, you are really having a day."

If only it were just this day.

I take off my other slipper and walk barefoot on the concrete, praying I still have some hand wipes from the rib place my brother and I went to last week stashed somewhere in my car. We're almost at the edge of the parking lot when I hear a crack as loud as thunder.

I glance up at the sky just in time to see a palm tree falling through the air. Benjie grabs my arm and we stare, openmouthed, as the tree lands with a sickening sound of crunching metal—right on top of my car.

———

"What are the odds?" Benjie says. He's standing beside me, surveying the damage to the old VW Golf I inherited from my dad. The roof is completely caved in, crumpled like an accordion underneath the thick trunk of the palm tree. It landed perfectly on my car, not a mark on either of the vehicles parked beside mine.

I wrap my arms around myself. What did I do to deserve this?

"Look on the bright side," Benjie says, putting his arm around my shaking shoulders. "No one was hurt."

"My car was hurt!" From the looks of it, it was totaled. It wasn't worth much, but it was mine, and there's no way I can afford another one.

This time, I don't even try to hold the tears back.

———

Benjie comes with me back to the hotel. While I stash Libby in my mom's office and clean the dog crap off my foot in the staff washroom, Marielle arranges to have the tree removed and my car towed. I think she's afraid I'll sue the hotel or something, because she offers to let me use one of the hotel's passenger vans until we've sorted the situation out.

Before she hands over the keys, Marielle reminds me that this is a company vehicle and whenever I'm behind the wheel, I'm representing the Grand Palms. Benjie is standing behind her and he rolls his eyes.

I chew my lip. "Don't I need a special license to drive the van?" The hotel has a fleet of cars that are much smaller and more manageable than the passenger vans.

"No," she says. "You just need common sense and I trust you to have that."

But she doesn't, not really, because the next thing she says is, "No running red lights or cutting anyone off."

Behind her, Benjie makes a face and wags his finger at me, back and forth, like a metronome. Normally, his spot-on impressions of Marielle make me laugh, but I'm not in the mood for any of it right now.

After saying goodbye to Benjie, I pick up Libby and take the elevator down to the underground lot. The van is parked in the far corner, exactly where Marielle said it would be. I jingle the keys, my palms sweating. She's given me one of the biggest vans, usually used to ferry large groups of guests to and from the airport. It's white, with the Grand Palms logo imprinted in gold on the doors.

I take a deep breath and climb inside, setting Libby on the seat beside me. I feel tiny behind the steering wheel, and it takes me a few minutes to figure out where everything is before I start the van.

My hands shake the entire ride home. I keep well below the speed limit, ignoring all the cars that pass me. When I pull up to my house half an hour later,

Ansel is loading his surfboard into the back of his beat-up truck. The waves are the only thing that ever gets my brother out of bed this early in the morning. His entire life is built around surfing. He's been taking a few classes at the University of Hawaii, but his attendance is spotty at best. It annoys me that he skips so much, especially when all I hear from my mom is how much college costs. The cost of it all was part of the reason I'd decided not to even bother applying. That, and I was so sure I'd be traveling with Nalani.

I turn off the van. Ansel walks over to me. He's wearing blue board shorts and a grungy pair of Adidas slides that I've begged him to get rid of. His red hair is sticking up in every direction.

He taps his fingers against the Grand Palms logo on the door. "Sweet ride. Where's your car?"

I'm in the middle of telling him what happened when he starts to laugh.

"What happened to your tooth?" he asks.

Libby lets out a plaintive yowl and my brother forgets about my tooth as he spots the black carrier resting on the passenger seat beside me.

He smiles. "Mom's going to kill you."

"She's not going to know."

"Marty, she's going to know," he says. "The woman doesn't miss a thing."

I rest my hand protectively on the carrier. "I just need to keep her here for a couple of days. Until I find someone who wants her."

Ansel shakes his head. "You don't need to convince me," he says. "It's Momzilla you need to worry about."

"If she finds out—which she won't—all she'll do is make me drop her off at a shelter," I say. "It's not like she's going to kick me out."

Ansel bends down to peek at Libby through the carrier's mesh window. "You best be quiet, cat, or it's curtains for you." He draws a finger across his throat.

"Stop."

His face straightens. "She's not going to let you keep her."

"I'm not planning to keep her," I say, but I know he can tell I'm lying. Ansel has always been able to read me. It's super annoying.

"I'll ask around," he says. "See if anyone's in the market for a new pet."

"Thanks."

Ansel walks back toward his van.

"Be careful!" I call. My brother isn't reckless, exactly, but surfing is a dangerous sport. No matter how good he is—and no matter what he thinks—he's not invincible. All it would take is one rogue wave and he could be seriously hurt. Or worse.

He turns around and gives me a thumbs-up, but his overconfidence doesn't make me feel any better.

———

Maybe Ansel got through to Libby, because she doesn't make a peep as I hurry through the house and downstairs to my bedroom. When I'm safely inside, I shut the door and unzip the carrier. It's not until she steps out and starts to explore my room, her long gray tail twitching, that I realize I don't have a litter box. Which seems like a pretty big oversight.

I open my closet door, like I'm somehow going to find one magically in there, stuffed in between my clothes and rarely used scuba gear. I'm wondering if there's a way I can somehow repurpose my laundry basket, when something falls from the top shelf. It clips me on the shoulder on the way down.

A shoebox that I could have sworn I'd buried at the very back of my closet is lying on its side. The lid has popped off, and everything I'd hidden in the box has spilled onto the floor. A pair of cherry-red sunglasses, a vanilla-scented travel candle, a hula-girl shot glass, and a luggage tag shaped like a surfboard.

All stuff I stole from guests at the hotel.

Looking at all of this makes me sweat. I kneel down

and pick up the sunglasses, trying to remember why I even wanted them in the first place.

Nalani knocked on the hotel room door. "House-keeping."

When no one answered, she opened the door with the master key card and we pushed our carts inside.

I groaned. The room was littered with pizza boxes and beer bottles. The duvet cover was in a puddle on the floor. The sheets were pulled off, showing the bare mattress. A bunch of snorkel gear was piled in the corner, along with an inside-out wetsuit. Haystacks of dirty clothes and towels were everywhere, and the teak floor was covered in sand.

"I'd like to nut-punch these slobs," Nalani grumbled as I gathered the dirty sheets into a ball and dumped them into the laundry basket attached to my cart.

I'd only been working at the hotel for a few weeks, but the state that some guests left their rooms in still managed to shock me.

After we remade the bed with eight-hundred-thread-count sheets, Nalani placed a couple of hand-towel swans in the middle of the bed, while I straightened a row of shiny black gift bags on the credenza. The bags were from one of the hotel's luxury stores, which meant that I could never afford whatever

*was nestled beneath the cream-colored tissue paper.
It bothered me that these people, whoever they were,
could buy whatever they wanted, whenever they
wanted, without sparing a thought for the price, while
pretty much everything I owned came from chain
stores in the Queen Ka'ahumanu Center mall. It wasn't
fair.*

*Next to the bags was a pair of red sunglasses. I
picked them up and slid them on. I'd been looking for
a pair just like this for ages.*

"They look good on you," Nalani said.

*It was just a pair of sunglasses. And these people
already had so much—they probably wouldn't even
notice they were missing. What was the harm if I took
them?*

I sit down on the floor, my heart racing. Nothing in
this box means anything to me. I didn't take any of
this stuff because I needed it—I took it because I felt
resentful of the people who could leave their rooms in
a disaster state and not spare a thought for the staff
who had to clean up after them. I was jealous of what
they had and I wanted to punish them in some small
way.

And all of a sudden I know why my luck has been
so bad. It has nothing to do with my dad leaving—and
everything to do with me stealing this stuff.

The universe is trying to settle the score.

I put all of the items back into the shoebox, handling them as gently as if they were grenades. This time, I don't bury the box at the back of my closet. I set it on my desk instead and sit down on my bed, wrapping my arms around myself.

I have to return all of this. It's the only way I'm ever going to get my luck back. And judging from how bad it's been lately, I need to do this sooner rather than later.

But it's one thing to know I have to give this stuff back. It's another to figure out *how* I'm going to do it. I only have a vague idea of which rooms I took each item from. On an average day, I'd clean ten suites, which were assigned at the beginning of each shift. I never wrote the room numbers down, because why bother? While housekeeping maintains a record of who cleaned which room on which day, I don't have access to those records.

But my mom does.

I take a deep breath. Breaking into her files might not earn me any points with the universe, but it's the only way I can get that information.

I just hope that it works.

Five

The dentist promised that the freezing would wear off in a few hours, but my mouth still feels numb when I arrive at work later that evening. I keep wiping at my lips, worried that I'm drooling. I could have called in sick, I guess, but I really want to get the information about the rooms I cleaned. I want to start sending these items back to their rightful owners and free myself from this curse of bad luck.

I've barely started my shift when Marielle walks up and thrusts a piece of paper into my hands.

"Marty. What is this?"

I glance down at the events rundown she asked me to create yesterday. We put them up in the elevators so guests know what's happening around the hotel. Yoga classes, hula lessons, a massage on the beach. A Maui Pubic Transit meeting.

Whoops.

"Maui *Public* Transit," Marielle says, tapping one red fingernail against the glaring typo. "This was up in the elevators all day!"

"Sorry," I mumble.

"Don't apologize; just do better," she says. She adjusts the brass name tag pinned on the pocket of her Hawaiian shirt, even though it's already perfectly straight. Benjie swears this a tactic to draw attention to the MANAGER title listed under her name when she's about to ask you to do something you're probably not going to want to do.

And sure enough . . .

"Now, I've been meaning to talk to you about something else," she says. "I need you to show some children of our VIP guests around the island. Take them to a luau, go to the beach, visit the aquarium. Whatever kids like to do."

I stare at her. She wants me to babysit?

"Wouldn't they be better off with a nanny?" I ask. The hotel has a roster of wonderful, caring *trained* nannies—why is she asking me, someone with zero experience with kids, to do this? I have no idea why she thinks I'm the right person for this job. It makes no sense.

Marielle's lips tighten, the only indication that she's heard my question. "I'll arrange for luau tickets for tomorrow night. And don't worry about your front desk shift—I'll find someone to cover it." She turns on her sensible black heel before I dare ask her anything else, and disappears through the doors into the back room.

I put my head down on the counter.

"Wait," Benjie says. "She's going to pay you to do all sorts of fun touristy stuff and you're pouting?"

I lift my head to glare at him. "This is going to be a million times harder than working the front desk."

"You are such a negative Nelly," he says. "People the world over take care of kids every single day. You'll be fine."

"I'm glad you think so."

"I know so. You'll be sipping mai tais while you're entertained by fire dancers and hula girls. I'm the opposite of sorry for you."

Well, when he puts it that way, it doesn't sound so bad.

Later that evening, after playing three rounds of Hangman—all of which I lose—Benjie goes on his second coffee break. I'm finally alone behind the front desk, so I decide to use the opportunity to see if I can break into my mom's files.

I glance behind me, just to make sure no one else is around, before I type in her password. My mom uses her birthday for everything, even though I've lectured her a hundred times about changing it to something harder to crack. For once, I'm glad she didn't listen to me.

A quick search of my name in the scheduling software turns up more than four hundred results. I suck in a breath. I can't believe I cleaned that many rooms in five months. How on earth am I going to figure out which of these rooms I took the stuff from?

Except . . . the only time I ever had the nerve to steal anything was when I was working with Nalani. Maybe if I type her name alongside mine . . .

The list immediately narrows down to 110 results. My shoulders relax a tiny bit. One hundred and ten is better than four hundred, for sure, but it still seems like an impossible number to try to wade through.

I'm nervous that Benjie could come back at any minute, so I save the record and send it to my email, then delete the email from my mom's sent box to cover my tracks. I'm busy setting up our next game of Hangman when I spot Will Foster crossing the lobby.

My fingers tighten on my pen as I watch him head toward the yellow leather club chairs. He's carrying a white Grand Palms mug and a book. Will must feel me looking at him, because he glances over and our eyes meet. Something inside me flutters as he reroutes and starts walking toward me.

My palms are sweaty. I'm usually a lot slower to warm up to someone, but something about Will really affects me. The way he smiles at me, like he's really glad to see me, like he's been waiting to talk to me, makes my heart race.

He probably smiles at everybody like that.

I hate the thought that he smiles at anyone else like that.

"Marty, hey," he says. He's tall and thin, a lamppost of a boy in plaid board shorts and a washed-out *X-Files* T-shirt. His dark hair is messy and standing high on his head, completely defying gravity. He sets his mug and book—a worn copy of *Ready Player One*—on the counter.

"You're still awake," I say. And then my face reddens because, hello, obvious.

"Can't sleep. Still on East Coast time, I guess." He runs a hand over the stubble sprouting on his jaw. There are dark purple circles under his eyes that weren't there when I saw him last night.

I tap my pen against his mug. "Might help if you weren't drinking coffee so late at night."

"It's probably not the best idea," he agrees. "But the coffee here is so good."

It's my turn to talk but he leans forward, resting his elbows on the polished bamboo counter, and my mind goes blank. He's inches from me, close enough that I can smell the coconut pomade he uses in that unruly tangle of hair. I twirl the pen in my fingers. Talking to people is my job—it's never been a problem for me before. But other people are not Will. And they're not usually staring at me so intently, with mesmerizingly deep blue eyes.

The silence between us lengthens to the point of awkwardness.

I clear my throat. "We grow our own beans."

My face burns. We grow our own beans?! God. What is wrong with me?

But instead of stopping and salvaging my dignity, I keep going. I can't seem to stop myself. "In Hawaii, I mean," I add. "We're one of only two states in America that grow coffee plants. The other is California."

I'm having an out-of-body experience. I can see myself delivering the most boring lecture ever on the history of Hawaiian coffee—who even knew I knew so much about the subject?—but unbelievably, Will doesn't run away. In fact, from the way his face lights up, it seems like he actually might be interested in this conversation.

"I'm planning to try every coffee place on the island," he says. "I don't want to go to the same place twice."

"Wow, you're really into coffee," I say. "Maybe you should open your own shop."

He drums his fingers against the counter. "That's the dream."

"I can give you a list of some of my favorite places, if you like."

His smile widens. "That'd be great."

"Have you been to Maui before?"

Will shakes his head. "My parents sent me as a graduation present," he says. "Of course, they made me bring my brother, so in reality, it's really a gift for them, too. Now we're both out of their hair for the summer."

My smile tightens. My mom took me out for dinner to celebrate, which is not nothing, but it doesn't exactly compare to an all-expenses-paid vacation. But then, I don't think there is much in my life that compares to Will Foster's.

He glances around the open-air lobby, at the high ceilings and marble columns, the indoor reflection pool with a stone mermaid at the center. "It must be amazing to live here. Like being on permanent vacation."

This is something tourists say all the time. It's hard for them to believe any different, when they're faced with the crash of waves against the shore and air scented with plumeria flowers. Their real lives, with all the day-to-day worries and problems, are thousands of miles away. My problems—even if they're mostly all of my own making—are still here.

"I don't have anything to compare it to," I say. "I've never left."

Will blinks at me. "Wait, what? You've never been off this island?"

"Well, I've been to the other Hawaiian islands. I just haven't been to the mainland." Hawaii is pretty remote—like thousands of miles from anywhere else on Earth—and we've never had the extra money to travel.

The pen I've been spinning in my fingers suddenly flies out of my hands. I make a quick move to grab it while it's still midair, which turns out to be a bad decision, because my elbow connects with Will's mug. I knock the mug over and coffee spills all over his book.

He snatches the book up, but it's too late—it's soaked.

"I'm so sorry." I grab a handful of tissues from the box we keep under the counter and try to wipe the book off, but it's no use. Coffee has leaked through the cover and onto the pages.

"Not a big deal," he says. "I've read it a million times anyway."

Marielle picks that moment to return to the front desk. She frowns at the sight of me mopping up coffee from the counter.

"Mr. Foster," she says, a practiced smile spreading over her face. "Everything okay?"

Marielle is very good at her job. She makes it her business to know as much as she can about our high-profile guests, so of course she knows who Will is. She probably knows more about his family than he does.

"It's fine. I just knocked over my coffee."

I shoot him a grateful look and finish cleaning up. It's nice of him to take the blame—I don't need Marielle yelling at me again tonight.

"I see you've met Marty," she says. "Good news. She's agreed to show you and your brother around the island."

My brow furrows. My mind spirals back to our conversation earlier this evening when she told me the "other duties as assigned" in my job description included babysitting rich kids. Only, now that I think about it, she didn't actually tell me how old the kids were.

Marielle's job is to make sure that our super-rich guests are kept happy. The only way she would have ever agreed to lend me out as a tour guide, rather than one of her other, more trusted staff, is if Will asked for me personally. And from the way his face is turning red, it's pretty clear he did.

"I thought you might like to go to a luau, so I've arranged for tickets tomorrow night," Marielle says. "How about you and Hayes meet Marty at the front entrance at five p.m.?"

"Great," Will says. He raises his eyebrows slightly at me. "I guess I'll see you tomorrow, then?"

I nod.

Marielle waits until Will has disappeared from the lobby with his soggy book before fixing her sharp gaze on me.

"Remember, you're representing the hotel," she says.

"Of course."

What she's really saying, without really saying it, is that Will Foster is off-limits. But she doesn't need to remind me that fraternizing with guests is against company policy. Will's only here for the summer. He may have requested that I show him around the island, but that's all I'm going to be showing him.

After what happened with Kahale, I'm through with boys. And no matter how hot Will Foster is or how zingy he makes me feel, he's not going to make me change my mind.

Six

Early the next morning, I'm walking out of the hotel, anxious to get home and comb through my list to see if I can jog my memory about which of the rooms I stole from, when I almost bump into Nalani. She looks like she just rolled out of bed and pulled on her housekeeping uniform.

"Ugh, you're so lucky you get to leave," she says, dragging her hair into a ponytail. "I have eight solid hours of cleaning pubes out of bathtubs ahead of me."

I frown. I'm not sure if Nalani's endgame is to make me feel guilty that I'm no longer in the trenches with her, but it works. Every time.

"But eyes on the prize, right?" she says. "Only a few

more months and we'll be out of here. Speaking of which, we really need to book our plane tickets."

My mouth is dry. My promotion to the front desk may have created a crack in our relationship, but that crack is going to widen into a gulf when Nalani finds out I'm not going to California with her. Putting off telling her isn't going to make her any less mad at me, but I can't drop this on her right before she's about to start her shift. Then again, I'm not sure there's ever going to be a good time to tell her. So maybe I should just do it and get it over with.

"Right," I say, swallowing. "About that—"

Nalani glances at her phone. "Crap, I'm late," she says, backing down the hall. "Text me later and we'll figure it out, okay? And don't forget about the party on Saturday."

Despite Nalani's reassurances that Kahale won't be there, I'm still nervous about going to the party at the rental house. There's too much overlap in our friend group for him not to have heard about it. And while I'm pretty sure that Kahale's been taking steps to avoid me, too, I can't be sure he'd turn down a party just because I'm going to be there.

I don't like thinking about him or what happened on prom night, so I box up the memory and push it down with all the other emotions I'm not ready to deal with, way down deep where hopefully it will collect dust and never bother me again.

I walk out to the parking lot. Someone in a red Jeep has parked too close to the hotel van. I can't get the driver's-side door open, so I go in through the passenger side, cursing as I awkwardly climb over the console. Once I'm settled, I start the van and pull out of the lot. It still feels unwieldy, especially when I'm trying to turn, but I'm starting to get used to driving it.

At this time of the morning the streets are pretty quiet, but there's usually a few people out for a stroll or jog, getting their exercise in before the sun fully rises and it gets too hot. I'm a few miles away from the hotel when I spot a familiar figure walking on the sidewalk, in the same plaid board shorts and T-shirt he was wearing when I saw him a few hours ago.

Will.

Marielle's not-so-subtle warning about keeping things professional is still ringing in my ears, along with my own promise to myself to not get involved with him. The smart thing would be to ignore all these feelings churning inside of me, the ones that aren't going to lead anywhere, and drive right past him. But that's not what I do. Instead I pull the van over and roll down the window.

"Did you get any sleep at all?" I ask him.

Will glances over at me, startled. The circles under his eyes are even more pronounced.

He walks over to the van and leans in the open window. "Not much," he says, giving me a tired smile. "And since I was up, I figured I'd get started on my quest. There's a coffee place a few miles from here that's right on the beach."

"Mahalo's," I say.

He drums his fingers on the side of the van, as if noticing what I'm driving for the first time. "Are you still working?"

"No. I'm having car trouble, so the hotel let me borrow the van for a while."

His fingers start drumming faster. "In that case . . . do you want to come with me?"

I chew my lip. Marielle didn't specifically say I couldn't hang out with Will outside of the time I'm paid to do it, but there's no way she would approve. However, she's not here—and what she doesn't know won't get me into trouble.

"Sure," I say. "Just let me park."

I pull down a side street, hoping that no one from the hotel will spot the van. I wish I'd changed before leaving work—I'm still in my uniform. I take off my name tag and drop it in the cup holder, then shake my hair out from its ponytail so it falls in dark waves over my shoulders. Then I feel silly, because this isn't a date. I don't know what it is, exactly, but it's definitely not a date.

Will's standing where I left him, his hands stuffed into the pockets of his shorts. He watches me come toward him, rocking back and forth slightly on his feet. His shock of dark hair adds a few extra inches to his already towering height.

He clears his throat. "So I probably should have mentioned that I asked your boss if you could show me and Hayes around," he says. "I hope that's okay."

I smile. "It's okay. In fact, I should probably thank you—you got me off nights. For a little while, anyway. "

The wind rustles through the palm trees as we start down the wide sidewalk that leads past a row of luxury hotels, each one bigger and fancier than the last. It hits me that the last time I walked down here I was with my dad. When I was a kid, he'd take me on an adventure every weekend. By the time I turned ten, there wasn't an inch of this island we hadn't explored.

I don't want to miss my dad, but when I'm faced with the memory of things we used to do, I can't help it. When he left, it knocked the wind out of me and I haven't yet caught my breath.

Will moves close to me to let a jogger pass. "Do you always work the night shift?"

"Yeah." I don't tell him that I used to work in housekeeping, because I don't want him to ask me any questions that might lead to me spilling my terrible secret. I can only imagine what he'd think of me if he found out I stole from guests. Although it can't be any worse than what I think about myself.

"My mom caught me sneaking out of the house a few months ago," I say. "She works for the hotel too, and making me work nights was the best punishment she could think of." But I guess that punishment is over, now that Marielle has reassigned me. At least temporarily.

The jogger is long gone, but Will is still walking close to me. "What happens when school starts?" he asks. "You go back to working the night shift?"

"It won't matter. I'm taking a gap year."

Something that looks a lot like envy flashes across his face. I know he probably thinks that gap year equals traveling, not working at the hotel—and not too long ago, that's what it meant to me, too.

"That sounds a whole lot better than business school," he says.

"You don't want to go?"

He shakes his head. "Whether I want to or not, I'm

going. Following in my dad's footsteps has always been 'the plan.' His plan, anyway," he says. "My entire life has already been mapped out for me."

I don't think that sounds so terrible. There's something comforting about knowing exactly what the future has in store for you. Especially when my own future seems a bit murky.

He winces. "I sound like an entitled douchebag, right?"

I shrug. It is hard to feel sorry for him. Plenty of people would kill to be in his place, to have the world laid out at their feet.

"It's just . . . sometimes I wish I had the freedom to do what *I* want, you know? Instead of what's expected of me."

"What would you rather do instead?"

"Live in a yurt in Israel. Climb Kilimanjaro. Run with the bulls in Spain. Open a coffee shop on a beach somewhere."

"What would happen if you told your dad you didn't want to go to school?"

He lets out a breath. "Trust me, I've tried. He doesn't want to hear it. And I'm not really in a position to argue with him at the moment," he says. "My grandfather left me some money and I'm supposed to get it when I turn eighteen in a few months, but my dad manages the trust fund. If he doesn't think I'm able to handle it—and it's pretty clear that he doesn't—then he can keep it from me until I'm twenty-five. So I have to behave and follow his direction." He holds his fist in the air. "Wharton or bust."

For all that I complain about my parents, they've never attached any strings to anything or tried to push their opinions about what I should do with the rest of my life onto me. When I told them I was taking a year off to travel, my dad was thrilled. Unlike my mom, who's lived on Maui most of her life, he arrived here after college. Hawaii was supposed to be a stopover on his way to Australia, a great way to kickoff the year-long backpacking trip he'd been planning since high school. But then he met my mom, and Australia became just a dream.

I know he'll be disappointed when he finds out I'm not going anywhere. But since he's part of the reason my plans have changed, he can't say much.

Will and I walk down the stone path that leads to Mahalo's, a thatched-roofed coffee shop set right on Wailea Beach. It's a busy place, and almost all of the white wicker chairs are taken by tourists who rolled out of bed extra early to watch the sun come up.

"What can I get you?" Will asks me, joining the line. The café smells strongly of roasted coffee beans and baked goods, thanks to a platter of cinnamon rolls on the counter.

I'm not sure where him buying me coffee falls— date or not date?—but I tell him I'd love an iced vanilla latte.

While he's ordering, I notice an elderly man preparing to leave his table in the far corner. I race across the restaurant to grab it, plunking down in one of the wicker chairs. I kick off my slippers and bury my feet in the cool sand. Wailea Beach is postcard perfect, an unobstructed view of pink-and-gold sky, and blue waves crashing against the shore. A few boats—mostly yachts—bob in the water.

It's a view that people pay a lot of money to come and see, but I'm more interested in watching Will. He's chatting with the girl behind the counter, seemingly unaware that he's holding up the line with his questions. He finally decides on which coffee to order and pulls out a black credit card, the kind that's only available to the extremely wealthy. Those cards are a pretty common sight in Wailea, and I'm not at all surprised that he has one. After the girl punches in his order, he walks over to wait for our drinks at the end of the counter.

I study his profile, his strong, almost hawklike nose and those full lips, that tornado of dark hair. The corner of his mouth curls up slightly as he smiles at the barista. He asks him about the big silver espresso machine, craning his neck around to watch the guy prepare his drink.

A few minutes later he carries our drinks over to the table.

"Hard to choose, but I went with the macadamia nut latte," he says, setting my boring vanilla latte in front of me.

"Thank you."

Will settles into the chair across the table from me and gazes out at the endless stretch of water. "So what do you do when you're not working?"

"The usual stuff," I say, which I know is not really any kind of an answer. "What do you want to do while you're here? Besides hit up every coffee shop?"

"Surfing, for sure. I'd also like to check out the volcano at some point." He narrows his eyes. "By the way, I see what you did there. You somehow turned the conversation back to me."

My cheeks start to heat up. Deflecting personal questions is my superpower—no one ever calls me on it. For some reason, Will seems genuinely interested in getting to know me.

I fiddle with my straw. I know I shouldn't compare him to Kahale, but it's hard not to think about the last time I let someone in. And what happened when I did.

Will takes a sip of his latte, waiting for me to respond, but the words are stuck in my throat. There's nothing exciting about my life, no way to spin working at the hotel forever into an interesting story. I wouldn't blame him if he gave up on me altogether, but instead he puts down his mug and leans toward me.

"Okay, how about we play a game?" he says. "Would you rather be covered in scales, like a dragon, or have whiskers, like a cat?"

I blink at him. "Um, neither."

He smiles and shakes his head. "You have to choose. That's the game."

"And what, exactly, is this supposed to tell you about me?"

"Well, I guess . . . whether you'd rather have scales or whiskers," he says. "And who wouldn't want to know that?"

"Okay," I say, smiling back at him. "Whiskers. At least then I could pluck them out."

"Nope. They'd grow back instantly. You'd never be rid of them."

"I stand by my answer," I say. "My turn. Would you rather wear a clown costume every day for a year or clown makeup every day for an entire year?"

"Would I have to wear one of those red noses?"

"Of course."

"Technically that's not makeup," he points out.

"If my whiskers grow back, then you definitely have to wear the nose."

He lets out a deep breath. "I'm going to have to go with the clown makeup."

I start to laugh.

"You're picturing me in the nose, aren't you?" he asks.

"Maybe."

He laughs too, and I start to relax. This conversation makes no sense—this game makes no sense—but it's fun.

"Okay," he says. "Would you rather only be able to listen to polka music for the rest of your life or one song—any song you like—over and over again, forever?"

"The same song."

"Well, now I have to ask what it is."

I frown. I should have known he'd ask a follow-up question. I could give him any song, other than the one I'm thinking of, but I feel like that would be cheating in some way, so I decide to take a chance and go with the truth.

"'Africa,'" I say.

"*It's gonna take a lot to drag me away from you,*" Will sings in a terrible, off-key voice. "*There's nothing that a hundred men or more could ever doooooooo.*"

I laugh.

He gives me a goofy smile that makes my heart turn over. "And now it'll be in my head for the rest of my life," he says. "Why that song, by the way?"

"My dad used to sing it to me when he'd put me to bed." Even when I got too old for him to tuck me in at night, he'd stand at my door and sing me to sleep. "It always made me feel so safe. Like nothing bad could ever happen."

Like he'd never leave.

"I can see why you'd pick that over polka," Will says.

"My turn," I say. "Eat a plate of sushi that's been left out in the hot sun or drink a glass of spoiled milk?"

He wrinkles his nose. "Is the goal of this question to make me throw up? Because I think I'm about to."

"It's strictly hypothetical. You don't have to actually do it."

"I guess I'll go with the sushi," he says. "If I drank rotten milk, I'd never be able to have cereal again and then what would be the point of living?" He leans back in his chair, stretching his legs under the table. His knee nudges mine and I'm pretty sure it's not an accident.

My stomach flutters. I want to be friends with Will, but all this getting-to-know-each-other feels like more than friendship. It feels like something bigger, which is the exact opposite of what I need right now.

I shift my leg so our knees are no longer touching. Will takes a sip of his latte, his eyes never leaving my face.

"Okay, me again," he says. "Would you rather live two hundred years in the past or two hundred years from now?"

"Two hundred years from now, for sure."

"I don't know, I think it would be interesting to live in a time before technology," he says. "Before everyone's noses were stuck in their phones."

"There was also polio and slavery and women didn't have the right to vote."

He makes a face. "I never thought of that. I change my answer."

"Too late." I swirl my straw in my cup, knocking the ice cubes together. "You're stuck in the 1800s now. Working as a blacksmith, worrying about getting cholera."

"Why would I be a blacksmith?" he says. "Can't I be

a gentleman farmer or run the general store or something?"

I smile. "Nope."

"All right, well, the good news is if I ever time travel back to the 1800s, my tenth-grade metalworking skills will finally be put to good use."

I haven't laughed this much in . . . I don't know when. A long time, anyway. So when Will's knee touches mine again, I don't move away. Even though this is a bad idea. Probably the worst idea.

"Speaking of the future," I say. "Would you rather be able to see everything that's going to happen in your life or go back and change one thing in your past?"

Will stiffens. His face tightens and he glances away from me and out to the ocean.

I swallow. Why did I ask him about the future? He already told me that his life has been laid out for him— he can already see what's going to happen. I know he feels trapped, but it's hard to feel bad for him, all things considered.

Still, I want to take back the question and restore the lighthearted mood, but I don't know how. I wish we'd never started with this stupid game.

"Change one thing," Will says finally. His eyes return to mine and he smiles, but it seems forced.

I wonder what it is about his past that he'd change,

but it's pretty clear from the way he's tapping his fingers against his coffee mug that he doesn't want to talk about it. And so we talk about the best place to get tacos on the island instead.

And that's pretty much how it goes, with small talk about hot sauce, until I put us both out of our misery and tell him that I need to get home.

Seven

I've been holed up in my room ever since I returned from my coffee date, or whatever that was, with Will. I've spent most of the afternoon with Libby in my lap, combing through the long list of shifts Nalani and I worked together. I know I took the sunglasses the first time we worked together—which happened to be the week after my dad left—but I'm not sure which of the ten rooms we cleaned that day is the correct one. Right now the idea that I'll be able to return this stuff feels impossible.

I need to give my brain a rest. I set Libby on the floor and head upstairs.

"Did you unload the dishwasher?" Mom calls as I pass by her room.

"I was just on my way to do it," I say. This isn't true—I was actually going to get a snack—but why poke the bear?

I peek into her room. My mom is standing behind a mountain of clothes piled high on her bed.

"What are you doing?" I ask as she grabs a worn gray cardigan—my dad's favorite sweater—from the pile and shoves it into an already overstuffed black rubbish bag.

"I'm finally getting around to cleaning out the closet." She snatches up a fistful of my dad's ties, including the burgundy-and-yellow striped one I gave him for Father's Day the year we discovered we both belonged in Gryffindor, and deposits them in the bag.

Tears sting my eyes. Giving away his stuff feels so final. He's been gone for almost half a year; I should be ready for this. But while I haven't forgiven him for leaving, I guess a secret corner of my heart is still hoping this is all just a bump in the road and that he'll change his mind. That he'll wake up and remember the family he left behind and come back to us.

I walk into the room and pick up one of his shirts. It's a plain blue T-shirt, nothing special, but it still smells like him. "What are you going to do with all of this?"

"Toss it." She sniffs, which is when I realize she's

been crying. I feel a stab of sympathy. She's normally so stoic, keeping a tight reign on her true feelings about the divorce hidden from my brother and me. It's easy to forget that she's heartbroken, too.

I think about keeping the shirt, but in the end I change my mind and shove it in the bag. No point hanging on to stuff he didn't want.

"Any word about your car?" Mom asks. Her dark hair is woven into a thick braid that swings over her shoulder like a pendulum when she leans over to grab a Kleenex from her night stand.

"It's totaled." The garage where Marielle had it towed called me this morning. As I suspected, the cost of fixing it is much more than it's worth. I have the hotel van until insurance pays up, and I can only hope that the settlement is enough to buy another car. It's pretty difficult to get around the island without one.

I hold open another rubbish bag so my mom can drop an armful of boxer shorts inside.

"Seriously, he didn't even take his underwear?" I say.

She grimaces. "He was in a pretty big hurry to get out of here."

My chest tightens. I knew that my parents weren't happy—it was impossible to be around them and not know that. They fought all the time. But I guess I figured that, happy or not, they'd find a way to make it work. After all, we were a family. So when the end actually came, it was a shock. To everyone but my dad, I guess. By the time he left, we were already in his rearview mirror.

I haven't talked to him in months, even though he's left me a bunch of messages. I don't get past the sound of him saying my name before I delete them. At this point, I don't know what would fix our relationship, but I know it goes beyond some lame apology left on my voice mail.

After we finish loading every last piece of my dad's old life into the bags, I help Mom cart them down the hallway and to the front door. She's going to donate everything to the thrift store tomorrow. Someone might as well get some use out of this stuff.

An hour later we're in the kitchen making dinner, when Ansel comes home. He's dirty and rumpled from working all day at the golf course.

"Howzit. What's with all the bags by the door?" he says, snatching a chunk of the red pepper I've just sliced.

I dart a glance at my mom, but I can tell from the way she's pointedly studying the mangos in the bowl on the counter that this is not a conservation she's anxious to have with my brother. Lately he's a fuse, just waiting to be lit—especially when it comes to my dad.

"We cleaned out Dad's closet," I say, like it's no big deal.

Ansel narrows his eyes. "So, what? You're just going to throw his stuff out?"

"There's no reason to keep any of it." Mom grabs a mango from the wooden bowl on the counter and gives it a squeeze, a little harder than is probably necessary.

"What if he wants it?"

"If he wanted it, he would have taken it with him." She rinses the fruit and then carefully runs a peeler over the rind. She's still avoiding looking at my brother. I'm not sure if it's because she's trying to keep his anger from escalating or because he is the spitting image of my dad and it hurts too much.

"What if I want it?" Ansel says, his lip curling. "That didn't occur to you?"

"Suddenly V-neck sweaters and boat shoes are your style?" I'm trying to lighten the mood, but it's a mistake. My words are like gas on a fire.

Ansel's face turns red. "Shut up, Marty," he says. "I can't believe you helped her with this. Actually, I take that back—I can believe it."

I'm trying not to take his outburst personally. Of the three of us, Dad leaving has hit Ansel the hardest.

He's somehow convinced himself that Mom drove him away—like if she'd just laid off him a little, he'd still be here. My mom is intense—we've all felt the need to run away from her at some point—but my brother has conveniently forgotten that Dad wasn't the easiest person to live with, either. He is not a saint. He's the worst mansplainer, he never listens, and he always, always puts his own needs first.

Case in point: he moved away and left his kids behind.

She doesn't answer Ansel—what is there to say? She just keeps peeling the mango, like nothing is wrong, but I can see her hands are shaking slightly.

He snorts in disgust, then storms out of the kitchen. I hear the rustle of plastic as he lifts the bags and carts them down the hall. A second later his door slams shut.

I think about going after him, trying to smooth things over, but then I hear my mom start to sniffle again. Our relationship may not be easy, but I can't leave her. Not now and not when the summer ends.

I know she would only argue with me if she found out I'm not planning on traveling with Nalani anymore. I don't want her to try to change my mind. And so, like with everything else I'm not ready to deal with, I push it aside. Hoping that it will all somehow magically go away.

Eight

The next day, I arrive at the hotel half an hour before I'm scheduled to meet Will and his brother for the luau. I was hoping to sneak behind the front desk so I could log in to the computer and check the guest records, but there are too many people around for me to safely do it, so I decide to use the computer in my mom's office instead. She's not working today, but if anyone asks me why I'm in her office, I can just tell them she asked me to pick something up for her. And pray they don't mention it to her.

Housekeeping is quiet—most of the day staff has left—and I make it to my mom's office unnoticed. I'm shaking a little as I sit down in her chair and log in to her computer. After I search through the first few guest records, I start to feel discouraged. There's nothing beyond the normal room service and movie charges, nothing that can tell me which room I took the sunglasses from.

But then, in room 5618, I find more than $15,000 worth of charges from some of the hotel's high-end stores. And that's when I remember the row of shiny black bags on the credenza.

I bite my lip. This has to be it.

My fingers fly across the keyboard. The room is registered to Jefferson and Lucy Miller and, thank god, we have their address on file. They live in Richmond, Virginia.

I'm smiling as I take a quick photo of their address, wondering what the Millers are going to think when they open a package postmarked from Hawaii and find a pair of sunglasses they probably never even noticed they were missing.

I turn off my mom's computer and head upstairs. Marielle asked me to check in with her, and I'm pretty sure it's because she wants to make sure I'm dressed appropriately. She gave me strict instructions on what to wear tonight. Something "conservative and classy." I'm not sure my yellow dress is going to cut it—especially because it's a little tighter and a little shorter than I recall it being—but it was the only thing in my closet that came anywhere close to her requirements.

It's happy hour and the lobby is crowded with people spilling out from the bar, clutching their half-price lava flows. Marielle is watching over the festivities from behind the front desk. She frowns, taking in my dress, as I cut around the line of guests waiting to check in.

Without a word, she slips off her gauzy white cardigan and holds it out toward me.

I blink at her.

"Take it," she says, shaking the sweater at me. "It's going to get cold once the sun sets."

That's not why she wants me to wear her cardigan and we both know it. But I reluctantly pull it on. It's too big and it smells strongly of her rose perfume. I feel my nose start to itch, like I'm going to sneeze.

"Remember—" she says, straightening her name tag.

"I know, I know," I interrupt. "I'm representing the hotel."

"Yes. Well." She pats me on the arm. "Have fun."

Fun. I'm not so sure about that. My nerves are in shreds. I don't know how this is going to go, considering what happened yesterday when Will and I played that stupid game. Plus, while my luck has held out so far today, I keep waiting for something bad to happen. Because something bad *always* does. However, I'm hoping that my intention to return everything is enough for the universe to cut me some slack tonight.

I head toward the hotel entrance. I spot Will kneeling by the indoor koi pond, watching a huge orange fish skim the surface of the water. He glances at me and smiles, and my heart speeds up.

I really wish my heart wouldn't do that. As much as I like him—there's no point denying it; I do like him—Will Foster is a complication I don't need. Spending the summer with him isn't going to be easy. Even if I was open to a relationship—which I am not—I don't want to feel these feelings for someone who lives on the other side of the ocean. I don't want to feel these feelings for anyone.

"Hey, Marty." Will stands up. "You look nice."

I smile. I know this is probably just good manners—something he says to all the girls—but my cheeks flush. I can keep telling myself that nothing can happen between us, but the fact is, I spent a lot more time than normal getting ready for tonight. I'm happy that he noticed.

"Thanks," I say. "So do you."

And he does look good. So very good. His dark hair

is in its usual mile-high pompadour, but one stray lock has fallen over his eye. He's wearing khaki shorts and a polo shirt, but instead of the tiny polo player on a horse, his shirt has Marvin the Martian embroidered on the pocket.

"Where's your brother?" I ask.

Will's face tightens almost imperceptibly. He gestures to a leather wingchair on the far side of the lobby, where the dark-haired boy I've seen before with Will is sprawled, scrolling through his phone.

"I needed a minute away from him," Will says. "I need a lot of minutes away from him, if I'm honest. This trip isn't off to the greatest start."

What am I walking into the middle of?

Hayes doesn't look up from his phone as we approach. Will knocks him lightly on the shoulder and he sighs heavily and gets to his feet. He's probably around fifteen. Tall and thin, with the same dark hair and the same startling blue eyes as his brother. He's dressed like Will, too, only his Polo shirt is the real deal and he's got on red-and-green slide sandals that probably cost more than my entire paycheck.

"Marty, this is Hayes."

"This thing isn't going to be all families and old people, right?" Hayes asks. There's a haughtiness in his expression that immediately puts me on guard. I know his type—I cross paths with people like him every day here at the hotel. The kind who expect to be treated like royalty, who think my sole reason for existing is to serve them.

"This 'thing' is a luau and it's going to be fun," Will says.

Hayes rolls his eyes. "We have very different ideas about what's fun."

"That is definitely true," Will replies.

My smile feels frozen on my face. I really hope they aren't going to argue all night. "We should probably get going."

The luau is held in the Imperial Wailea, one of several high-end properties that line the same stretch of perfect sugar-sand beach as the Grand Palms, but it's just far enough away that we need to drive. I lead them out into the parking lot, past a row of luxury cars, including a very shiny red BMW convertible that Hayes stops to admire.

When I stop in front of the hotel van, he mutters, "This is a joke, right?"

A bolt of irritation shoots through me. I've done my fair share of complaining about the van, but now I feel weirdly defensive of it.

"No joke," Will says.

Hayes frowns. "Why can't we rent a car?"

"I already told you, you have to be twenty-five," Will says, sounding tired. "The van is fine."

"Fine for you, maybe," he huffs.

I jingle the keys, looking back and forth between them. The tension in the air is thick and I have no idea how to cut it.

Will slides open the door. "Just get in."

I'm surprised when Hayes complies—although he is muttering under his breath as he climbs into the backseat. He moves over, clearly expecting his brother to sit beside him—leaving me alone up front like a chauffeur—but Will slides into the passenger seat instead.

"What kind of name is Marty, anyway?" Hayes asks. I narrow my eyes at him in the rearview mirror. He's rolled down his window and his elbow rests on the open sill.

What kind of name is Hayes?

"It's short for Martina," I say, pulling onto a wide street lined with palm trees. "It was my grandmother's name."

She died right before I was born. My dad always said that our name wasn't the only thing we shared, that I'm also as bright, talented, and thoughtful as she was. I'm not sure he'd still believe that if he found out

I'm a thief. Then again, my opinion of him isn't what it once was, either.

Thinking about my dad can quickly torpedo my mood, so I push him out of my brain.

"So, Hayes, Will mentioned you want to do some surfing," I say. I can probably convince Ansel to give them lessons—if he's still talking to me, that is. I haven't seen him since he stormed out of the kitchen when he found out Mom and I were getting rid of Dad's stuff.

Hayes snorts. "My brother came here to surf. I'm only here because my parents forced me to join him."

Will's jaw tightens. "Who complains about a trip to Hawaii?"

"Whatever," Hayes says. "You don't get it. And I don't care what we do, as long as it isn't touristy."

O-kay. Well, we're on our way to a luau, which is pretty much the most touristy thing to do on the island. I've been to a few of them over the years, when family from out of town was visiting.

Will and Hayes continue to bicker until I pull up to the Imperial Wailea. I hand the valet my keys and we walk through the front door. Like the Grand Palms, this hotel has a huge open-air lobby that maximizes the spectacular view of the Pacific Ocean framed by swaying palm trees.

We head toward a bamboo arch and join the line to get into the luau. While we wait to check in, a girl in a traditional Hawaiian mu'umu'u approaches us with leis.

"Aloha. Welcome to the Imperial Wailea Luau." She steps toward Hayes and he bends slightly so she can loop a string of fresh plumeria flowers around his neck.

"Hey, I just got lei-d," he says, snickering.

I wrinkle my nose. Will must also be experiencing secondhand embarrassment, because he groans and says, "How many times have you heard that gem?" to the girl.

She smiles, but she doesn't comment and I see myself in her—shrugging off the same dumb comments and tired old jokes, day after day, because she has to. It's part of the job.

"Oh, come on," Hayes says as she gives Will and me our leis. "That was funny."

The line moves forward. When we reach the front, another girl takes our names and then leads us under the bamboo arch and along a crushed seashell path. The luau is held on a stretch of emerald-green grass on the edge of the beach, partially hidden by a row of palm trees. The sun is just beginning to set, painting the sky pink and orange. The hostess leads us to a table right near the stage, where a well-built guy in a green pareo is playing "Over the Rainbow" on a ukulele. The smell of roasting meat wafts through the air, courtesy of the kālua pig in the fire pit.

Just after the hostess seats us—I take the seat between Will and Hayes—a family with two small kids plunks down in the empty seats at our table. Hayes rolls his eyes as the mom clears a spot on the table to set down a coloring book and crayons for the two girls.

A waiter arrives with a tray of mai tais. The drinks are served in coconut shells with little pink paper umbrellas. Hayes grabs one of the coconuts and takes a sip. "Hey, Will. These drinks are virgin. Just like you."

Will tosses his paper umbrella at him, his cheeks turning red as Hayes pulls out a tiny bottle of rum that he must have taken from the hotel's minibar.

"Do you think that's a good idea?" Will asks him.

"It's the only way I'm going to get through this evening." Hayes dumps half of the alcohol into his drink then holds the bottle out to his brother.

"No thanks."

"Right. I forgot. You're no fun anymore," Hayes says. "One bad experience and you swear off alcohol forever."

"I learn from my mistakes."

Hayes turns to me and smiles. "That's a dig, Marty, in case you missed it." He offers me the bottle, but I shake my head. I wouldn't mind something to steady my nerves, but I'm driving.

He grimaces. "So you're no fun, either." He dumps the rest of the bottle into his drink.

"Might want to pace yourself," Will says.

"Don't worry about me," Hayes replies.

"I wish I didn't have to."

The guy on the stage starts to play Elvis's "Hawaiian Wedding Song" on his ukulele. His chest is bare, showing off his well-toned abs. A haku lei encircles his curly dark hair.

"So, Marty," Hayes says, drawing my attention back to the table. "What kind of perks do you get, working at a hotel?"

"I guess the perk would be my paycheck."

"Hayes is planning to live off his trust fund," Will says.

Hayes tucks his paper umbrella behind his ear. "Isn't that what trust funds are for?"

"I wouldn't know," I say, but my words are drowned out by the sound of someone blowing a conch shell. Two men dressed in pareos, leis looped around their necks, carry the metal tray containing the roasted pig right past our table.

Hayes pales. "I can't eat that. It has a face."

"So did that steak you had for lunch," Will points out.

"Yeah, but I didn't have to look it in the eye."

"You don't have to eat it," I say sharply. I've reached my limit with Hayes and his constant complaining. "There's plenty of other food."

The line for the buffet is already starting to form, so we stand up and walk over to join it. The kālua pig is the centerpiece of the table, slightly raised and surrounded by pineapple rings. Bamboo bowls filled with Hawaiian food—taro rolls and lomi-lomi salmon, chicken luau, and fried rice—cover every inch of space.

"What is this purple stuff?" Hayes asks me, his nose wrinkling as he pokes distrustfully at a bowl of poi with a spoon.

"It's poi," I say.

He stares blankly at me.

"Poi is made from taro." Will scoops some onto his plate. "It's kind of like a potato. Just try it."

Hayes shakes his head. "Nah, I'm good."

By the time we reach the end of the table, all Hayes has added is a baseball-sized scoop of macaroni salad and a dinner roll.

The family across from us is already halfway

through their meal when we sit back down. While we eat, the drums kick up and a procession of Hawaiian dancers carrying lit tiki torches weave through the tables to the stage. Hayes can't tear his eyes away from the hula girls with their shaking hips and coconut shell bikini tops.

I'm distracted by the fire dancers with their flaming batons, and because I'm not paying attention, the spoonful of poi I intend for my mouth slides off my spoon and onto my chest. I gasp as it drips into my cleavage and all down the front of Marielle's white sweater.

Hayes snickers. Will hands me a napkin and I dab at the purple-gray blob, but it just makes the stain worse. My breath quickens. How am I supposed to tell my boss I ruined her sweater?

"I'll be right back," I say. I run to the bathroom inside the hotel. I slip off the cardigan and run cold water over the mark, but it's no use—this isn't coming out. I glance up at my frazzled reflection in the mirror, my wild eyes and pinched lips, and I almost laugh at how crazy I look. *You're blowing this way of proportion*, I tell myself. *Marielle isn't going to fire you for this.*

I don't think so, anyway.

I close my eyes and take a deep breath. In and out. In and out. And when I open my eyes again, I feel a bit calmer.

There's nothing else I can do about the sweater right now, so I clean the rest of the poi off me and then slip the damp cardigan over my arm. I'll take it to a dry cleaner tomorrow; maybe they can work some dry-cleaning magic. In the meantime, I'm going to try my best to enjoy the rest of the evening.

When I leave the bathroom, I find Will waiting for me at the end of the corridor. My heart skips. He's leaning against the wall, hands stuffed into the pockets of his shorts. Watching me walk toward him.

"I wanted to make sure you're okay," he says.

"I'm fine. It's just a sweater."

Hopefully Marielle feels the same way.

"Sorry about my brother," Will says. "He can be a real dick sometimes. But I'm sure you've picked up on that already."

I give him a small smile. "He's not so bad."

He totally is, but there's really nothing to be gained by agreeing with Will. At the end of the day, Hayes is his brother. And I'm just some girl he met a few days ago.

"It's just . . . he's going through something right

now," he says. "I've been trying to cut him some slack, but he's making it *really* hard."

I'd like to ask Will what's going on with Hayes, as well as what's keeping him up at night, but I'm not sure that's a line I want to cross. Keeping Will at arm's length is already difficult, especially when he's standing right in front of me, his eyes locked on mine. The way he's looking at me, like he wants to close what little distance there is left between us—like if I just gave him a signal, he'd kiss me—makes my breath come in shallow bursts. My legs start to shake.

How can I want to be close to him and as far from him as possible at the same time? It's super confusing. I take a step away from him before something happens that we can't take back.

"Our dinner's probably getting cold," I say. I wrap my arms around myself. It's better not to start anything with him. I know this, but I'm still disappointed.

"Yeah," Will says quietly. "I guess we should get back."

We haven't been gone long—the fire-knife dancers are still onstage—but clearly it was long enough for Hayes to polish off two more mini bottles of rum. The empty bottles are scattered on the table near his head, which is resting inches from his still-full plate. The family we were sitting with has disappeared. Maybe they're getting dessert or maybe they asked to be seated somewhere far away from this stupidly drunk kid.

Will swears under his breath. "Hayes," he says, poking his brother hard on the shoulder.

Hayes sits up. Macaroni salad clings to the front of his hair. His eyes are unfocused and he's having trouble holding his head up, like his neck is made of rubber.

"We need to get him to the hotel," Will says to me.

"I'm fine," Hayes slurs.

But this is not what fine looks like. People at the surrounding tables are staring as Will and I help Hayes to his feet. Hayes's head lolls against his chest as we awkwardly walk him through the luau. We're almost at the van—I've already taken my keys out of my purse—when Hayes mumbles something.

"What?" Will says.

Hayes suddenly pulls away from us and hunches over, his hands on his knees. And then he throws up.

All over my feet.

Nine

After what happened last night, it's pretty clear that Karma is not going to let up. Not until I return all the stuff I stole, at least.

Will was mortified that his brother puked on me, but there's no way he could have been more embarrassed than I was. I chucked my shoes in the garbage—the second pair I've had to get rid of in the past few days, due to disgusting circumstances—and went back to the hotel bathroom to rinse myself off with hand soap.

When I got home, I took a long shower. I went to bed early, but I didn't sleep well. I kept waking up, wanting morning to arrive so I could send the cursed sunglasses back to the Millers. Which is why, just before nine a.m., I'm sitting on the front step of the post office, waiting for it to open.

There's no one else in the parking lot. The sky is overcast but it's humid, and I'm already starting to sweat. I take out my phone. Will and I texted back and forth a bunch during the night—I'm not the only one who had trouble sleeping—and I've agreed to meet him for coffee this morning. Just him. Not that Hayes would be in any shape to go out, anyway.

I hope he is spectacularly hungover.

I know I probably shouldn't go out with Will this morning—I need to establish some boundaries if I'm going to keep things strictly professional between us, and that definitely doesn't include hanging out with him every day. But . . .

I sigh.

That *but* is the problem. Because I like him. And I want to see him. Meeting him has been literally the only good thing to happen to me this summer. Of course, if you look at it another way—that I've met a guy I'm interested in who seems to return my feelings, except he's going to leave in a few weeks—maybe it's not such great luck after all.

Maybe this is just another joke the universe is playing on me.

The rain starts to come down. I get off the curb

and stand under the red awning above the post office door. I still have a few minutes before it opens, so I do something else I really shouldn't do: creep on Will's Instagram. I find his profile. I know it's his, even though his account is locked down, because his profile photo is of Marvin the Martin. I smile, wondering if I should follow him, but I chicken out. I don't want him to know I've stalked him on social media.

Since I'm already in Instagram, I decide to lurk on Kahale's profile. My hands start to shake as I scroll through a bunch of photos of him posing shirtless on the beach, until I get to the one I'm searching for. A photo of the two of us, taken on prom night. Kahale and me, standing beside the lemon tree in his parents' backyard. He's wearing a white linen suit; I'm in the sparkly midnight-blue halter dress that I bought because it reminded me of the galaxy. I'd never spent so much money on a single piece of clothing before, but it made me feel beautiful, so I figured it was worth it.

My throat tightens. I remember how much I was looking forward to the night ahead and to being with this boy I'd had a massive crush on forever, the one who finally, *finally* seemed to return my feelings.

I can't believe he hasn't deleted it. But then, it appears he doesn't delete any of his photos, because following that post are pictures of him and Grace Hamasaki, the girl he ditched me for right in the middle of prom. They broke up two weeks later, but she's still all over his feed.

I've tried my best not to think about Kahale going MIA at prom, searching for him all over the hotel and then discovering him with Grace, making out in the backseat of the limo he'd brought me to the dance in. Or the days after, when he kept texting me, trying to apologize.

"Don't you dare text him back," Nalani said as we pushed our housekeeping carts down the hallway. We'd just started our shift, but all I wanted to do was climb back into bed and hide under the covers. I hadn't been out of the house in two days.

"I'm not planning to," I said, wiping my hand across my eyes. Kahale kept texting me, hoping we could still be friends, but I couldn't imagine how we could ever go back. Well, maybe he could, but I certainly couldn't.

"You shouldn't be wasting any time feeling bad about him," Nalani said. "Let Grace have him. We both know you can do much better."

Maybe that was true, but it didn't make it hurt any less. I'd had a crush on Kahale since freshman year. I was so happy when he asked me to the dance. It wasn't that easy to just let go of my feelings, as much as I wished I could.

Nalani stopped in front of our first assigned room. After knocking on the door and getting no answer, she slid the HOUSEKEEPING PLEASE sign off the door handle and inserted her master key. We pushed our carts into the room.

At first glance, the suite didn't even look like it needed to be cleaned. There was barely a trace of the person staying there, aside from a stack of paperbacks and a travel candle on the nightstand. They had even made the bed. Two twenty-dollar bills rested on the pillow.

Nalani grinned. She picked up the bills and fanned herself with them.

"Why did they want us to come in here if there isn't anything to clean?" I asked her. We had half an hour allotted to clean this room and nothing to do. Not that I was complaining.

"Why ask why?" She walked over and opened the closet doors. A row of men's clothes hung on wooden hangers; a few pairs of polished leather loafers were lined up on the floor.

"He's here alone," Nalani said. She pulled out a crisp white button-down shirt and held it against her. "Must be a businessman."

"Probably here for a conference."

We sometimes played a game where we tried to figure out who the guest was, based on their personal items.

I decided to check the bathroom, just in case he needed clean towels or more toiletries.

"Nalani," I called, my stomach lurching. "Can you come in here?"

She walked in, still holding the white shirt in her hand.

"Seriously?" She held the shirt over her nose and stared at me, wide-eyed.

"I guess we know why he left us a tip," I said.

Guests were always quick to call the front desk when they had a problem with their room, even if it was for something as minor as a burned-out lightbulb, but for whatever reason, the guy staying here didn't feel the need to give us a heads-up that he'd clogged the toilet. Unspeakably dirty water had overflowed onto the marble floor.

"I'm never going to unsee this," Nalani said, backing out of the bathroom.

Gagging, I grabbed a stack of used towels and threw them on the floor, hoping they would absorb the worst of it. Then I went back into the main room and called down to housekeeping to let them know we were dealing with an apocalypse.

"Leo's coming up," I told Nalani.

She stuck the white shirt haphazardly back into the closet and started rooting through the hotel minibar. She grabbed two mini bottles of rum and a tin of macadamia nuts and stuck them in a drawer on her cart.

I lifted up the travel candle from the bedside table. It was practically new—the wick had been lit, but barely any of the wax had melted. It smelled like vanilla.

The guy may have given us a tip, but it didn't feel like nearly enough to make up for the catastrophic mess he'd left behind. And maybe it was because I was tired of people messing with me and not thinking twice about it—like my dad, like Kahale—so I took the candle.

I didn't need it—or even want it, really. I took it because it seemed like a fairly harmless way to mete out justice to someone who I felt deserved it. I didn't feel great about stealing it, even as I was taking it. It didn't give me a rush or make me feel better. I didn't feel anything.

And that might be the worst part.

I tap my finger against my lip. Leo would have logged the issue of the clogged toilet into this guy's guest record. So all I need to do is look through the records for the ten rooms Nalani and I cleaned that day—two days after prom—and I should be able to find the right room. Which means I can return the candle.

My shoulders relax. I glance at the guy behind the post office door as he unlocks it and lets me inside. I'm about to close out of Instagram, when my finger slips and I accidently like that photo of me and Kahale. I gasp. I quickly unlike it, praying that he doesn't get a notification. Because if he gets one, he'll know I've been on his profile.

And I really don't want him to know I was on his profile.

I stuff the sunglasses into a padded envelope and pay to send them back to Richmond, Virginia. It costs a bit more than I expected, but the relief I feel when I drop them into the mailbox is worth every penny.

———

"Howzit, Marty," Leo says as I park beside his baby-blue moped in the staff lot. "What are you doing here so early?"

"Back on day shift," I say. Sort of.

I tell him about Marielle's assignment. If he thinks it's weird that she's hired me out as a tour guide, he keeps the thought to himself.

I roll up the window and climb out of the van. Leo unbuckles the strap of his helmet and pulls it off, then stows it in the cargo space under the seat of his moped. He grabs his lunch bag and we walk toward the hotel together. I notice that he's limping a little and it worries me, but I don't ask him about it—Leo doesn't like questions about his health or when he's going to retire. He's worked at the Grand Palms for almost forty years, but he doesn't seem to be in any hurry to leave, and I'm super glad about that.

"Found a home for Libby yet?" he asks.

"Not yet."

His face brightens.

"Don't get excited," I say, before he can list all the reasons why I should keep her. "I just haven't had time to find a place for her."

Leo's smile tells me that he doesn't buy it. "Your mom will come around."

If he believes that, then he doesn't know her at all.

The hotel comes into view and I spot Will near the entrance to the lobby, standing beside a marble column. I thought about asking him to meet me at the coffee shop, but then I realized that I'm paid to be his ride. Friends or not, I'm on the hotel payroll and I'm supposed to show him around.

"That him?" Leo asks.

I nod.

He purses his lips. I know he feels protective over me, even more so since my dad left. But there's really nothing to worry about.

"We're just friends," I say, but I don't sound convincing and Leo gives me a skeptical look.

I squeeze his arm. "I know better than to get involved with a guest."

Leo shakes his head. "I sure hope so."

Will glances over and notices us staring at him. I nudge Leo down the path that leads to the staff entrance.

"Okay, I can take a hint," he says with a laugh. He tells me to be good, then disappears down the path. I stand there awkwardly, suddenly unsure of what to do with my hands, as Will walks toward me. I pull my long hair into a messy topknot—my dad used to make fun of me when I put it up like this. He called it a doorknob.

I hate that he invades my thoughts when I'm least expecting it. He's left three messages in the past few days—all of which I deleted without bothering to listen to them. Just thinking about him makes me cranky, and so I do what I always do and push him away.

"Hey," Will says when he reaches me. The circles

under his eyes are somehow even more pronounced, and I feel guilty for keeping him up texting last night.

"How's Hayes?" I ask.

He grimaces. "He finally stopped throwing up," he says. "Sorry, again, for what happened."

"It wasn't your fault." The person who should be apologizing is Hayes. But I'm not holding my breath for that.

"So," Will says. "Where is this place with the magical coconut cappuccinos?"

During our late-night text session, I told him about this place I used to go to all the time. I wasn't lying about the coconut cappuccinos, but they're mostly known for having the best loco moco on the island and I really want breakfast.

"It's a few miles from here," I say. "You up for a walk?"

"Always."

We head away from the hotel. It's rush hour, which in Wailea just means there are a few more cars on the road than normal. It's already starting to get warm, so I slide off my pink hoodie and tie it around my waist.

"I think we should continue our game," Will says. He's walking faster than I am—his legs are a lot longer than mine—and he slows his pace so we're in step. "I've thought of a million more questions I want to ask you."

I'm kind of surprised he wants to play again, considering how this went the last time, when I asked him if he'd change something about his past. But I'm willing to try again. I'll just have to be more careful about my questions.

"Okay," I say. "Let's see what you've got."

"Would you rather live to be a thousand or live to a hundred, ten times?"

"You mean live the same life, over and over again? Like *Groundhog Day*?"

He shrugs. "Sure, let's go with that."

"Ten lives, I guess," I reply. "I can't imagine I'd hold up that well if I lived to be a thousand."

He laughs. "Fair point. Although I think repeating the same life over again would be boring as hell."

"Yeah, but it'd be like having a do-over. You could fix your mistakes."

A shadow passes over Will's face, and I want to stuff the words back into my mouth. So much for being careful.

"Well, that would be handy," he says finally.

I could just ask him what it is he'd want to change— it's obvious that something happened in his past that is bothering him. But if he really wanted me to know, he'd tell me. It's easier to just change the subject and move us to safer territory.

"Would you rather be locked in a closet with a boa constrictor or a dozen rats?" I ask him.

"Rats," he says without hesitation.

I squeal. "Really?"

"Why? You'd pick the snake?"

"Definitely."

"But the snake could kill you," he says. "The rats might bite you, but they probably wouldn't cause any lasting damage. Unless you contracted the plague or something. And who gets the plague nowadays? I'll tell you who: no one."

"I'd still take the snake."

"No one ever picks the snake," he says.

"I just did."

I hate the thought of him playing this game with someone else. With some other girl, back in his real life. The life he's going to return to at the end of the summer.

"All right, my turn," Will says. "Invisibility cloak or the Marauder's Map?"

"Marauder's Map." It sure would have saved me a whole lot of trouble when sneaking out of the house and avoiding Kahale.

"I think I'd take the invisibility cloak," he says. "There are plenty of times I've wished I were invisible."

It's hard to imagine Will, with his seemingly perfect life, feeling this way. And it's not lost on me that we hardly ever agree on anything. But even though these questions are ridiculous, he was right—they are a good way to learn about someone.

"Moving on," I say. "Never be able to stop dancing or have to sing everything?"

"Singing."

"Me too! Then life would be like a musical." I clap my hands.

He sighs. "I change my answer."

"You can't change your answer!"

"Says who?"

I nudge him with my elbow and he laughs.

We've reached Island Coffee. It's a shabby, nondescript little place, sandwiched in the middle of a strip mall. A very different vibe from the coffee shop on the beach we went to the other day. Gus, the owner of the place, is obsessed with the Beatles, and the entire shop is plastered in the band's vintage posters and record album covers. Behind the counter, there's even a glass case containing an Island Coffee mug that Gus claims Ringo Starr once drank out of.

"Hey Jude" is playing when we walk in. We're the only customers. Gus glances at us from the wooden stool he's perched on behind the counter. "Aloha, Marty. It's been a while." He stands up and leans on the counter, smiling so wide that his eyes crinkle at the corners. "How's your dad?"

I swallow. It's impossible to escape the memories of my dad when he's everywhere I turn on this island. He used to bring me here all the time when I was a kid. I'd get a hot chocolate with extra whipped cream and we'd sit outside on the veranda, even though there wasn't much to look at but the cars coming in and out of the parking lot.

"He's good," I say. And I'm sure it's the truth. Whatever life he's made for himself on Oʻahu, it must be better than the one he had here. After all, it was worth leaving his family for.

"Well, you tell him I said hi," Gus says. "Now, you want the usual?"

I nod. "And two coconut cappuccinos, please."

"What's the usual?" Will asks as Gus punches our order into the cash register.

I smile. "You'll see."

Will tries to pay, but I insist on buying. He only relents when I tell him that the hotel will reimburse me. We go and sit at a table near the back, underneath the famous poster of the Beatles walking across Abbey Road. "Hello, Goodbye" is playing now, and I can just make out the hiss of the espresso machine over the music as Gus makes our cappuccinos.

"So, that guy said you come here with your dad," Will says, resting his elbows on the table. "I know your mom works at the hotel and that you have a brother, but you've never mentioned your dad before."

I glance away from him. I haven't really told him anything about my life—not anything important, anyway—but that's on purpose. It's better if we keep things surface level. I don't want to go deep with another person who isn't going to stick around. And Will isn't permanent.

And while he may think he wants to know more about me, I doubt that includes hearing all about my parents' breakup and my dad abandoning us. Will's on vacation—he's here to have fun, not be brought down by my sad backstory.

"There's not a lot to tell." I fiddle with the four-leaf-clover charm on my necklace, zipping it back and forth on the chain.

Will looks at me expectantly, his eyebrows raised. So I guess I'm not getting off the hook that easily.

"My dad left six months ago," I say, shifting in my seat. "I don't talk to him."

"Like, ever?"

I shake my head.

Will winces. "I'm sorry."

"It's okay," I say. "I'm over it."

It's really the furthest thing from okay—and I'll never be over it—but what else is there to say?

Gus saves me from having to delve any further into this conversation by placing two huge plates, each containing a gravy-covered hamburger on rice with a fried egg perfectly balanced on top of the whole thing, in front of us.

"Loco moco," he says.

"Best on the island," I reply.

Gus also hands us blue mugs with a sea turtle detailed in the cappuccino foam, along with a bottle of barbecue sauce, then retreats to his stool behind the counter. I pick up my fork, ready to shovel my breakfast into my mouth if Will asks any more follow-up questions about my dad, but his attention is now focused on his plate.

"This smells amazing," he says. "Thanks for bringing me here."

I smile. I like that he's interested in seeing more of Maui, beyond the grass skirts and tiki torches. And I like that I'm the one who gets to show him the island.

I reach for the barbecue sauce and shake a generous

amount of it on top of my egg. Will stares at me, his brow furrowed.

"What?" I ask.

"I'm not sure how I feel about mixing barbecue sauce and gravy."

I laugh. "You don't have to. It's not required." In fact, I think I'm probably the only person, besides my dad, who eats it this way. "But you're missing out."

Will takes the barbecue sauce from me and adds some on his eggs. "I'm trusting you on this."

My phone beeps. It's Nalani, checking to make sure I haven't forgotten about the party tomorrow night. I don't really want to go, but she'll kill me if I don't show up. She's texted me a bunch of times about our trip over the past few days, and I haven't responded. I know she knows something's up. I sigh. I haven't found the right time to tell her I'm not going.

I'll tell her soon, I promise myself.

"Everything okay?" Will asks.

I turn my phone facedown on the table. It beeps a few more times, but this time I ignore it. "All good."

He cocks his head and stares at me until my palms start to sweat. I thought I was pretty good at keeping my emotions hidden, but he seems to see through me.

"My friend's throwing a party on Saturday," I say, "and—"

"I'm in," he interrupts.

I blink, taken aback. I was about to tell him that I'm not super into parties; I wasn't going to invite him. And I guess Will realizes he should have let me finish, because his cheeks flush.

"I mean, if you're asking," he says.

Introducing him to my friends, bringing him further into my life, is definitely not in the plan. But there's no way to tell him that without coming off totally rude—and besides, maybe bringing him isn't the worst thing. Especially because it means I don't have to show up alone. So I smile and say, "Yes, I was asking."

Will's shoulders relax. He polishes off his loco moco before I'm even halfway through mine, and when I see him eyeing my plate, I push it toward the center of the table so we can share.

Ten

You have to tell Nalani you're not going with her," Ansel says. "She's been blowing up my phone because you're not answering yours."

We're sitting inside a golf cart near the ninth hole, hidden behind the snack shack so the golfers won't catch sight of us. I can hear the thwack of balls being struck and the occasional curse as someone misses their shot.

"There hasn't been a good time," I say, chewing on my thumbnail. I'll be seeing her tomorrow night, at the party at the rental house, but I'm hoping she'll be too busy playing hostess to corner me about the trip.

My brother gives me a look. His feet are propped

up on the dashboard. His calves are covered in grass clippings. His main job is to trim the green, which means he spends most of his shift on the riding mower.

"While we're on the topic of avoiding people, you're going to have to deal with Dad too sometime," he says.

"I don't have anything to say to him." I cross my arms, like it's armor that's going to protect me from this conversation that I very much don't want to have.

"It's not all his fault, you know," Ansel says.

I snort. "He moved away."

"Come on, Marty. He's on O'ahu, not on the moon," he replies. "You need to cut him a break. He's trying."

"He's not trying that hard." Sure, he leaves a message on my phone a few times a week, but he hasn't come back to Maui to try to work it out with me in person. Like Ansel said, O'ahu isn't the moon.

My brother holds up his hands and I relax a little. For once, it seems that he's not in the mood to fight. He reaches for his phone, tucked into the cup holder on the dashboard. He scrolls through the screen and groans. "Aw man, the waves at Ho'okipa are sick right now." He turns the phone to show me the surf report.

The surf report rules his life. My mom doesn't get his obsession with surfing—she doesn't see it as anything more than an indulgent hobby, a distraction that takes up way too much of his time. But he loves it, so I wish she'd be more supportive. It might make things easier between them.

"I know of a couple of guys who are looking to learn." There are a million other instructors I could hire to teach Will and Hayes to surf, but I know my brother is good. And I know he could use the money.

Ansel drops his phone back in the cup holder. "I hate giving lessons."

"It's only for a couple of hours and it pays really well," I say. When Will told me what he'd be willing to spend, I considered giving him lessons myself. "They're nice guys."

Well, Will is, anyway.

"Fine," he says, sighing. "I've been thinking of getting back into instructing."

"What? You just said you hate giving lessons."

"I hate cutting grass more," he replies. "And I need a second job. I can't live in Mom's basement forever."

Ansel's almost twenty, so it shouldn't come as a shock that he wants to get on with his life, but I still feel blindsided. Just like when Dad left. Just like when Kahale ditched me at prom.

"I've got to get out of there, Marty," he says. He fiddles with the straight-from-the-seventies puka shell necklace his ex-girlfriend Jade gave him. He refuses to take it off, no matter how much his friends make fun of him for it.

"I can't believe you're going to leave me alone with Mom."

"Yeah, well, don't panic. You're stuck with me a little while longer." He starts up the golf cart. He pulls around the side of the building and onto the asphalt path that leads back to the clubhouse. The course is a brilliant emerald green with a few strategically placed palm trees that frame the endless blue ocean and the rise of Molokai in the distance. A group of golfers in Hawaiian shirts glance over at us. One of them raises his hand to catch my brother's attention, but Ansel pretends not to see him and steps on the gas.

"By the way, I heard your cat wailing this morning." He takes a corner a bit too fast and I reach out to steady myself on the dashboard. "Don't worry. I turned my music up so Mom wouldn't hear. But it's only a matter of time before she finds out."

I haven't even tried to find a home for Libby. The thought of giving her away makes me feel panicky. I'm still hoping I'll find a way to convince my mom to let me keep her.

"I'll find somewhere for her," I say.

Ansel just shakes his head.

"What are you doing?" Hayes asks later that afternoon as I bend down beside the hotel van. We're in the parking lot of my favorite restaurant, a little Mexican place in the middle of a strip mall in Napili.

"Find a penny, pick it up . . . ," I say.

He snorts. "That's just a dumb superstition," he says. "Besides, that's a quarter."

Maybe it is just a dumb superstition, but I'm not taking any chances. Ever since I lost my luck, I've picked up every coin I've come across and knocked on wood more times than I can count. I've responded to every chain letter that my aunt Kaye forwards to me, even though I've asked her not to at least a million times. And, okay, none of it has seemed to make much of a difference, but it hasn't hurt, either.

"I get it," Will says. He pulls a tiny red plastic telescope out of his pocket, the kind of cheap toy you'd get from a bubble-gum machine. "I've carried this for luck for years."

Hayes shakes his head. "There's no such thing as luck—good or bad," he says. "It's like believing in leprechauns. Or unicorns."

Will ignores him. "When we were kids, we spent the summers with our grandparents at their house in the Hamptons," he says. "My grandfather used to bury treasures for us in his garden. Rubber balls, plastic soldiers. Things like that. When he gave me this telescope, he told me that when I looked through it, I'd always be able to find him in the stars."

It sounds like such a happy memory, but Hayes's face has closed off. He storms away from us and into the restaurant.

"Our grandfather died a few months ago," Will says, watching him go. "He's having a hard time with it. And then some other stuff happened, too. It's just been a crappy couple of months."

I wonder if that "other stuff" is what has been keeping him up at night.

"I'm sorry about your grandpa," I say.

"Thanks."

We walk into the restaurant. It's decorated in green and red and white, the colors of the Mexican flag, and the whole place smells of cumin and garlic and chili.

Hayes is slumped at a table in the corner, looking sullen. I'm sure this place is far from what they're used to—sand on the floor and people eating in their bathing suits. It's as close to a glimpse of my real life as I've given them so far, and I suddenly feel nervous that they won't like it.

"So what's good?" Will asks me, studying the menu board above the cash register.

"Everything," I say. "But I usually go for the tacos."

"Can't go wrong with tacos."

Will places our order—nine chicken tacos, a basket of chips and salsa, and three bottles of pineapple soda. We have to wait for our number to be called, so we head over to the table. Hayes is tracing a finger over the map of Maui imprinted on the sticky tabletop. "We should go to Hana," he says, his finger stopping on the easternmost tip of the map. "Grandpa used to talk about how gorgeous it was. Remember?"

Will's eyebrows lift in surprise. "Yeah. He talked about Hana a lot," he says. "He said it was magical. Marty, would you be up for going there?"

Normally, I'd take a hard pass. Hana is at least a five-hour drive and while the scenery is breathtaking, the road is made up of stomach-churning switchbacks that never fail to make me carsick. But I'm supposed to show them around the island, so if they want to go to Hana, then I guess I'll take them.

"Sure," I say. "It'll take us a full day to do it properly, though."

"Cool." Hayes grabs a bottle of the hottest hot sauce from the little basket on the table and sprinkles way too much on his tacos. I'm about to warn him, but then I remember the stupid way he's behaved so far and the fact that he threw up on me. So, okay, maybe it's mean, but I let him take a big bite. Which probably isn't going to help my karma at all, especially because his face turns hot-sauce red and he starts to cough.

"You okay?" Will asks him.

Hayes's eyes are watering. He grabs his soda and chugs it, his Adam's apple bobbing in his throat.

And now I feel worse than I have since I started sending the stolen items back. Because if there's a lesson that the universe is trying to teach me—treat others as you would have them treat you, for example—obviously I haven't learned it yet.

Half an hour later we're standing on the beach, watching the sea turtles fight against the waves as they make their way to shore.

Napili Bay is quiet, a bit out of the way. My dad used to bring Ansel and me here sometimes. We'd stand on this same rock, watching the turtles bob in the water, and my dad would tell us that they were a family. They stuck together. Just like us.

Only that turned out not to be true.

"They come here every night?" Will asks.

I nod. "Right at sunset. Like clockwork."

Ten feet away, one of the turtles climbs out of the water and onto the same expanse of slippery black rock we're standing on. The turtle is about three feet long and, in the waning light, looks almost the same dark color as the rock.

"I didn't realize they were so big." Will takes a step toward it, holding up his phone to take a photo.

"From her size, I'd say this girl is probably at least twenty-five years old," I say. "Don't get too close. It's illegal to touch the turtles in Hawaii. Besides, she might bite if she feels cornered."

"How do you know it's a she?" he asks.

"Her tail. It's shorter than the male's."

The sky is beginning to darken. There aren't that many people left on the beach, just a few families packing up their gear.

"So what else is there to do on this island, besides eat tacos and look at turtles?" Hayes asks me. "Both of which, by the way, I can do back home."

"Really? You have sea turtles in Philadelphia?" When I think of the East Coast, I think of tall buildings and snowy winters and people in a big hurry to get where they're going. I don't know how sea turtles fit into that picture.

"Sure, in an aquarium in New Jersey," Will replies. "Not the same as seeing them in the wild."

"My point is that there isn't much to do, especially at night." Hayes bends down and picks up a rock. "Don't you get bored?" he asks me.

"No," I snap.

Maybe I shouldn't take it so personally, but Hayes and his complaining are getting on my nerves.

"It's just a slower pace than we're used to. Which is exactly why I wanted to come," Will says.

"No, you wanted to come because it's five thousand miles from home," he says. "But being here doesn't change anything. It's just a vacation from your problems. But guess what, Will? They're all still waiting for you back home. Sooner or later, you're going to have to deal with—"

"Hayes," Will says, a warning note in his voice.

My shoulders tighten. I know something about keeping secrets—there are things I keep to myself, things I don't want Will to know about me. Like the fact that I'm a thief. So I can't blame him for wanting to keep his.

Hayes snorts. He pulls his arm back and throws his rock like he's pitching a baseball, far into the water. He takes off down the beach. It's still light enough to track him as he walks along the shore, but the sun is setting rapidly. Napili isn't big, he's going to hit the end of the bay soon, but trying to find him in the dark will still be a pain in the butt.

Will swears under his breath. He follows Hayes, and I want to give them some privacy, so I head back to the van. Fifteen minutes later they climb inside without a word, and they remain silent all the way back to the hotel.

Eleven

I waited until my mom got home this afternoon before I left for the hotel. I've only been in her office for ten minutes, but I've already located the owner of the travel candle. As I expected, Leo left a note about the clogged toilet on Mr. Robert O'Reilly's guest record. The guy lives in Iowa and I'm guessing sending this candle back to him will cost me more than it's actually worth, but it must be done.

Now that I've figured out who the candle belongs to, I start to search for the owner of the hula-girl shot glass.

Here's what I remember: I took the shot glass during one of the last shifts that Nalani and I worked in housekeeping together. We were scheduled to work together four times in those last two weeks before I was promoted, which means the owner of the shot glass could have stayed in any one of the forty rooms we cleaned.

I sigh. And I sigh even harder after I search through all forty records and nothing jumps out at me. I put my head down on the desk, combing through my memory for any other details that might help me figure out who the shot glass belongs to.

An older man answered the door in one of the hotel's soft white bathrobes. He was wearing thick black glasses and his gray hair was unkempt, like he'd just woken up from a nap. He frowned when he saw Nalani and me standing in front of him.

"Sorry to interrupt, sir. Should we come back at a better time?" Nalani asked. The HOUSEKEEPING PLEASE *sign hung from the doorknob, but maybe he'd meant to flip it to* DO NOT DISTURB. *It happened a lot.*

"No, I'd like the room cleaned now," he said curtly.

He stepped back to hold the door open, and Nalani and I exchanged a glance. Clearly he was planning to stay in the room while we worked, something we both hated. This kind of guest would watch us closely, like they expected us to take something, or they'd pretend we weren't even there. Either way, it was uncomfortable.

The fact that all this guy was wearing was a bathrobe made me nervous, so I was relieved to see a blond woman in a purple bikini sunning herself on the balcony. The balcony overlooked the garden, which meant that this was one of the hotel's cheaper suites—although even the garden suites in the Grand Palms ran more than six hundred dollars a night.

I lift my head off the desk. That's it! The suite had a view of the garden, which means that the room was on the west side of the property. I pull up my schedule on my phone, my heart picking up speed. Two of the shifts that Nalani and I worked together were in the west wing of the hotel. I smile. I've just narrowed the list down to twenty possible rooms.

I bring up the list of rooms we cleaned during the two shifts. Six of them had children staying in them. There was no sign of any kids in that room, so I can eliminate those from the list. That leaves me with fourteen rooms. But none of the remaining guest records are showing me anything that brings me any closer to solving the mystery.

I don't have any more time to search, either, because I'm due to meet Will and Hayes in the lobby. I sigh. I have all sorts of feelings about taking the two of them to Nalani's party, but it's too late to back out now, so I guess all I can do is hope that I don't regret it.

For years, Nalani has been throwing parties in the rental houses her parents manage. Somehow we've never been caught, although maybe that's because she keeps the guest list small and won't let anyone leave until we've scrubbed all traces of our existence from the place.

Will is beside me in the passenger seat. His knee is bouncing up and down and he hasn't spoken more than a few words on the entire ride over here. Hayes is more subdued than usual, too. That same weird vibe from the other night is still there—it doesn't seem to have dissipated at all. Neither of them seems to be in a party mood, and my nerves ratchet up with each mile we get closer to the house.

I pull up in front of a tall gate and punch in the code Nalani sent me. The gate slowly swings open, revealing a sprawling white mansion that glows in the evening light. The house was designed by some famous architect whose name I can never remember, and it's situated on a rocky bluff that overlooks the ocean. It's like something out of a magazine.

"Now this is more like it," Hayes says.

I smile at him in the rearview mirror, then glance at

Will, expecting a similar reaction, but he just shrugs. "Nice."

Nice? That's it?

And maybe to him that's all this house is—I mean, he probably lives in something similar. Sometimes I forget that what's impressive to me is just run-of-the-mill for him. Still, I'm annoyed as we climb out of the hotel van. He's the one who wanted to come to this party in the first place.

Will stuffs his hands into his pockets, and the three of us walk along a stone path, toward the sounds of people splashing in the pool. The closer we get to the backyard, the farther behind me Will and Hayes drop, having a whispered argument.

"Hey, Marty?" Will says, just before we round the corner to the back of the house. "We'll catch up with you in a minute, okay?"

I don't really want to walk into this party by myself—this was part of the reason why I brought them. But I guess I don't have a choice. "Sure."

The night is still warm, even though the sun has set and the stars are out. The pool is lit up and I spot Nalani sitting by the side of the pool in a black-and-white polka-dot bikini, a red Solo cup in her hand. Half a dozen people we went to high school with are in the pool, playing water volleyball. A few others are gathered in the lounge chairs, near the built-in stone barbecue. The smell of burnt meat drifts on the late evening air.

"Marty!" Nalani calls. I start to walk over to her when, suddenly, the volleyball comes flying through the air and sucker-punches me in the stomach, knocking the wind right out of me.

I double over, my arms wrapping around my aching stomach. Tears spring to my eyes.

"Are you okay?" Nalani's beside me, her hand resting on my back.

I nod. I take a shaky breath and then straighten up. This type of thing—getting hit with errant volleyballs, palm trees falling on my car—never used to happen to me. At least, not with the alarming regularity that they happen now. It's Karma reminding me, once again, that I need to stop messing around and finish what I started.

"Whoops, sorry, Marty," Hunter calls from the pool. "I don't know how that happened. I was aiming in the opposite direction."

Wait. Hunter is here? I throw a panicked glance at Nalani. If he's here, then it means that Kahale is probably here, too.

"They showed up together," Nalani says quietly. "What was I supposed to do? Kick him out?"

"Yes!"

She shakes her head. "Marty, come on."

"Fine. But you could have at least warned me."

Her mouth tightens. "I would have, but you haven't answered any of my texts lately," she says. "Are you mad at me or something?"

"No. I just . . ."

I rub my stomach. The words should be easy enough to say—*I'm not going traveling with you*—but I can't seem to get them out. She'll want to know why, but I know she won't understand my answer. Nalani's spent the past few years dreaming about getting as far away from her parents as possible. Leaving my mom isn't an option for me. Not until she's in a better headspace, anyway.

This is a mess.

And, oh god, it's about to get messier, because now Kahale is climbing out of the pool. He's wearing blue board shorts and his chest is bare, showing off his well-toned abs and the intricate detail of the eagle tattoo on his shoulder. I'm shaking as Kahale grabs a striped towel from a stack near the edge of the pool and wraps it around his waist. My fight-or-flight instinct kicks in. I choose flight, but Nalani grabs my arm.

"You can do this," she says as Kahale starts to walk

toward us. She gives my arm a squeeze and then takes off before I can beg her not to leave me alone with him.

At one time, I would have given anything to have Kahale Mahelona go out of his way to talk to me at a party. We've been in the same friend group since junior high, but he never paid much attention to me. Not until one night, a few weeks before prom, when a bunch of us were at Keawakapu Beach for a bonfire. He sat down next to me and we talked the entire night. For the next few weeks we were inseparable. I thought we were on our way to becoming something really great. And then prom happened.

"Hey, Marty," Kahale says. He smiles, revealing the dimple in his left cheek, but if he thinks that's all it's going to take for me to forgive him, he is dead wrong.

I stare at him, expressionless, until the smile slips off his face.

He clears his throat. "I, uh, was hoping I'd see you here tonight. I've been wanting to talk to you."

"Oh yeah? What about?" I can feel everyone at the party pretending not to watch us. They were all at prom—they all know what happened—and I suddenly feel like I'm reliving the humiliation of that night.

Kahale's ears start to turn red. "About what happened," he says. "What I did . . . There's no excuse. You didn't deserve to be treated like that. I'm sorry."

He stopped trying to reach out to me a week or so after prom, when he finally clued in I wasn't going to answer his texts. We've been avoiding each other all summer, yet he shows up tonight, at this party he knew I would be going to. Why?

I stiffen. Oh my god. He saw my Instagram notification! He knows I was creeping on his account. He thinks it means that I'm feeling nostalgic or sentimental or that I want to be friends, when really, I was just bored/nosy.

I. Could. Die.

"Okay. Well, thanks," I say.

Kahale stares at me like he's waiting for me to say something else. "So . . . we're friends?"

I shrug. I'm not so sure about that. His apology seems sincere enough, I guess, but I can't imagine being friends with him again. I can, however, be civil.

"Okay, well . . . I'm glad that's resolved," he says, pulling out the dimple again. I'm relieved to find that it no longer has the same hold over me that it once did. Whether that has to do with the fact that I'm truly over him or that Will has entered the picture, I don't know. Either way, I'm glad my days of crushing on Kahale are over.

Someone cannonballs into the pool, sending an arc of water through the air that soaks the front of my shorts.

"Who the hell is that?" Kahale asks as Hayes surfaces, fully clothed, between Hailey and Anne-Marie, two girls from my chemistry class. Both of them are staring at him like he just farted or something.

"That would be my brother," Will says. He's come up behind me and he's standing close enough that his fingers brush lightly against mine. "He doesn't always think before he acts."

Kahale's eyes narrow. "And who are you?"

"Will Foster."

Kahale stares at Will's outstretched hand for a few seconds before shaking it. He looks from Will to me, then down at our hands, which are almost touching.

"Well. Nice talking to you, Marty," Kahale says before sauntering away.

"Your ex?" Will says as soon as he's out of earshot.

"Sort of." Kahale was never technically my boyfriend, but we were on our way to being together. At least, I thought we were.

Will drums his fingers against his thigh. "Is he the reason that you're so closed off?"

"Excuse me?" I wrap my arms around my waist, feeling like I've been sucker-punched again.

"It's just . . . you're kind of a hard person to get to know."

My face is hot. What he's saying isn't untrue, but I don't know how to respond. He's made it clear that he wants to know me, but I'm so afraid of what will happen if I let him see beneath the surface. I'm afraid of falling for someone who is eventually going to leave.

We watch Hayes awkwardly try to climb onto a swan floatie, the silence between us growing heavier by the second. The odds of this becoming anything real are small, but if I don't take the chance and let him in, I'll never know. What if wondering what could have been is worse?

I take a deep breath and rub my four-leaf-clover charm. "You want to go somewhere and talk?"

"Yeah," he says. "Sounds good."

I lead him down a path toward a pair of chaise lounges set on the edge of the bluff. There's almost no moon tonight, and the only light comes from a few flickering tiki torches and a sky full of brilliant stars. The sound of the party is swallowed by the roar of the waves crashing against the shore below us.

The salt air is cooler here by a few degrees. We lie down on the lounges and I kick off my slippers and dig my feet into the sand. I clasp my shaking hands together. I don't know how to start this conversation, to tell him who I am, so I go back to our game. Maybe that will ease me into it.

"Would you rather visit every country on Earth or go into space?" I sneak a glance at him. It's dark enough that I can't make out his features, but from the way his head is tilted, I can tell he's staring up at the sky.

"Space. Sci-fi geek, remember?" Will says. "You?"

"I'd see the world. Definitely."

"But you're going to, though, right? During your gap year?"

I let out a breath. This is it. This is my chance to let him in.

"Actually, I'm going to be sticking around Maui for a while."

"What? Why?" he asks. "I mean, it's beautiful here—I can see why you'd want to stay—but don't you want to see what else is out there?"

"Of course," I say. "But now's not the right time."

"What are you going to do instead?"

"Work at the hotel."

Will doesn't say anything. I can feel that he wants to ask more, but although I've opened the door a few inches, I'm not quite ready to kick it down yet. And I guess he senses that, because he says, "Zombie apocalypse or alien invasion?"

"Zombies. They're dumber than aliens. I could fight them off easier."

"But maybe aliens aren't our enemies."

"Not according to pretty much every sci-fi movie I've ever seen," I say.

The wind picks up and I curl up on the lounge, feeling myself start to relax.

"Stuck in a broken elevator with an ex-girlfriend or on a broken ski lift with Darth Vader?" I ask him.

He doesn't even hesitate. "The ski lift."

"Wow," I say. "You'd pick Darth Vader over your ex-girlfriend? Must have been a bad breakup."

"It wasn't great. But it was for the best. My mom always says, 'When someone shows you who they are, believe them.'"

"Is your mom Maya Angelou?" I ask. "Because I'm pretty sure she said that."

Will laughs. "No, she's not," he says. "But I do think she's pretty wise. She knows when to pull out the right quote, anyway." He reaches across the space between us and nudges my leg. "What about you? Elevator or ski lift?"

"Well, I've never seen snow, so I guess I'd go with the ski—"

Something suddenly swoops low through the air. I duck as it skims the top of my head.

"What the hell was that?" he yells.

"It was a bat." I shudder.

Will slides low in his lounge and wraps his arms over his head. "What? There are bats here?"

"They won't hurt you."

"It just flew at us!"

"It flew at *me*," I say.

"What if it was a vampire bat?"

"You know vampire bats aren't actually vampires, right?" I say as he slides off his lounge and motions for me to make room for him. I move over, my skin tingling, as he drops down beside me. The chaise isn't built for two—especially when one of us is so tall—and we have to shift around until we both find a comfortable position. We end up on our backs, Will's arms tucked behind his head, my head dangerously near his chest.

He's so close, in fact, I have to remind myself to breathe.

"So about that guy . . . ," he says. "Your 'sort of' ex."

I guess this is his way of asking about what happened between Kahale and me. I don't really want to tell him—being dumped at the prom is embarrassing—but this is why I brought him over here. So I could start being honest about my life.

I stare up at the stars, trying to slow my heart rate.

"He decided he was more interested in someone else. Right in the middle of prom."

Will lets out a breath. "Wow, that's pretty crappy."

"Yeah."

He's quiet a minute. I'm expecting another question about Kahale, but instead Will says, "Remember when you asked me if I'd rather be able to see my future or go back and change my past?"

"Sure."

He shifts, lowering his arms so they're resting on his stomach. "Last New Year's Eve, Hayes and I went to a party at my friend Toby's house. It was the week after my grandfather died, and we were both in a bad place. We got stupid drunk," he says. "Toby tried to convince us to stay over, but it was a nice night and we didn't live far from his house, so we decided to walk home."

His fingers start to drum against his abdomen. He's tense and I wonder if I really want to hear what he's about to tell me, this thing that won't let him sleep at night.

"I don't remember whose idea it was, but we decided it would be funny to steal the stop sign at the end of our street. It was just supposed to be a dumb prank, but when I woke up, my dad mentioned that there'd been an accident down the road." Will swallows. "I knew as soon as the words left his mouth that it was because we'd taken the stop sign."

I put my hand over his to stop it from jumping around. He turns his palm up and laces his fingers through mine. We're holding hands and while fireworks are going off throughout my body, I'm also worried about where this story is leading.

"Anyway," he continues, "because there was no stop sign, this guy—John—drove right through the intersection and right into a truck. He was hurt pretty badly."

My heart sinks. His fingers are still shaking a little and I squeeze them lightly. Will stares up at the sky, the endless expanse of stars.

"No one knew we'd taken the sign," he says. "Hayes completely freaked out. He didn't want anyone to find out what we'd done, but there was no way I could keep that secret. So I told my dad. He flipped, of course. Then he paid to keep things quiet, so my brother and I wouldn't get into any trouble."

"Is that why you're going to business school?" I ask him.

He nods. "I can't disappoint him again."

I'm impressed that Will was brave enough to step up and take responsibility for what he did. I've kept my secret to myself. Although I've been trying my best to make amends by sending the items I stole back, I wonder if it would have even occurred to me if my luck hadn't sucked so badly. Maybe that shoebox would have just stayed buried in the back of my closet. Maybe I would have eventually forgotten all about it or let myself off the hook, because really, who had I hurt? The stuff I stole was useless and the people I took from probably hadn't even noticed they were missing anything.

He's trusted me with his secret. I guess I should return the favor.

I close my eyes. "When I worked in housekeeping, I took some things from the guests," I say. "Not anything valuable, just dumb stuff, like a candle and a shot glass." I hope Will doesn't notice my palms are sweating. "But that doesn't make it right. I've been trying to track it all down and send it back."

There's a relief in telling someone, a lightening of the weight on my chest. Will squeezes my fingers, the same way I squeezed his a few minutes ago, and tears sting my eyes. For the first time in months, I feel like maybe everything is going to be all right.

And then, before the thought has even left my mind, the chaise we're sitting on collapses. Somehow the legs give out and we land with a thud. Our hands are still entwined, but Will's fingers are now digging into my skin and my butt aches as if I've been spanked.

"What the hell?" Will says.

Right—I forgot to tell him that I'm being punished by the gods.

"Are you okay?" He sits up just as the sound of someone yodeling cuts through the night air. I glance back toward the house. All the lights are on and I can see the outline of someone standing on the roof, about to dive off it and into the pool.

Will swears. "It's my brother. He yodels whenever he's about to do something dumb."

We scramble off the chaise and run toward the house. My friends are standing in a circle below, chanting at him to jump. All of them except for Nalani.

"You have to get him down," she says, wringing her hands. "He's going to break his neck! How am I going to explain that to my parents?"

"Hayes!" Will yells.

I gasp as Hayes looks down at him and almost loses his balance. He rights himself and takes a swig of whatever is in his Solo cup, then tosses the cup off the roof. It lands in the pool and a second later he follows it, only he's not nearly as graceful. He hits the water with a smack, sending a tsunami of water over the edge of the pool.

I hold my breath until he resurfaces, yodeling at the top of his lungs. Everyone cheers. Everyone except Will and Nalani and me.

Will sighs. "Maybe we'd better call it a night."

Twelve

I don't know what I was thinking, scheduling surfing lessons with Ansel the night after Nalani's party. The sun has barely brushed the sky when I pull up beside my brother in the Ho'okipa Beach parking lot. He's unloading his surfboard from his truck.

"Tell me why we couldn't have done this later in the day," Hayes grumbles. He's beside me in the passenger seat. His eyes are closed and he's pale, so he's clearly feeling the effects of last night's poor choices. We practically had to carry him out of the party.

Maybe it's evil of me, but I'm a little bit glad that he's not feeling well. The idea of Hayes being tossed around by the waves—and potentially tossing his breakfast—brings me great joy.

"It's less crowded first thing in the morning," I say. "And the wind is usually lower."

"Come on, Hayes. Get it together!" Will says from the backseat. He claps a hand on his brother's shoulder. "This is going to be great."

Hayes does not look convinced. He closes his eyes, making no move to follow us out of the van.

I hand my brother the coffee Will convinced me to stop for after I picked him up. Extra-large vanilla macadamia nut, Ansel's favorite.

"Please, just be nice," I whisper to him.

"I'm always nice," Ansel replies.

That is not even a little bit true. And, judging from the scowl on his face, he is in a mood.

Will comes to stand beside me. His hair is in its usual pompadour. He's wearing board shorts and a T-shirt that's molded to his body, highlighting his athletic frame and the ripple of his biceps. I suddenly feel very warm.

I threw on a long-sleeved white T-shirt over a turquoise bikini. My hair is tucked underneath one of my brother's wide-brimmed surf hats.

"You must be Ansel," Will says, holding out his hand. "Thanks for agreeing to this. Marty says you're the best."

Ansel studies Will before finally taking his hand. "You bring boards?"

Will nods. He leads us around to the back of the van and pops open the door to reveal the two electric-blue surfboards he rented, laid out on the folded-down rear seat.

"I hope these are okay," he says. "I haven't done a lot of surfing, so I didn't really know what to get."

"They'll do," Ansel grunts. He glances at the clunky black dive watch strapped to his wrist. "Let's get started."

Will raps his knuckles on the passenger-side window and startles Hayes awake. "Get moving."

Hayes groans, but he rolls out of the vehicle. His eyes are bloodshot and he stinks of alcohol.

We each grab our surfboards, tucking them under our arms. The board Ansel lent me is nine feet long and neon green, so bright that you could probably see it from space. It was his first board and he used it for years, so it's pretty thrashed. It looks so used, especially in comparison to the beautiful boards Will and Hayes are carrying, and I'm embarrassed, even though I know Will probably hasn't even noticed. And if he has, he doesn't care.

We walk down the tree-lined path that leads to the beach. As soon as we hit the sand, we kick off our slippers into a pile. Ansel drops his backpack, stuffed with towels and sunscreen, and after he gives Will and Hayes a quick brief on water safety, he instructs them to put their boards down a few feet apart from each other.

I settle on the ground, next to my brother's bag. Like Ansel, I practically grew up on a surfboard, so I can skip Surfing 101. I watch as the boys all lie belly down on the boards in the paddling position and Ansel demonstrates how to pop up.

Will catches on quickly and Ansel lets him sit on his board beside me while we wait for Hayes to get the hang of it. His balance is totally off and he tumbles off the board again and again, his face turning redder with each attempt. When he finally manages to do it three times in a row without falling, Ansel declares him ready to try it in the water.

Hayes stares out at the ocean, the crashing waves pounding against the shore. "Wasn't there a shark attack on Maui a few months ago?"

"Not at this particular beach," Ansel says, picking up his board. "Well, not recently, anyway."

Hayes rolls his bottom lip between his thumb and his forefinger. From the look on Ansel's face, he's losing what little patience he has—the waves are calling to him and he wants to be out there. He claps one of his big hands on Hayes's shoulder and gives him a shake. "Listen, you're more likely to die from being kicked in the head by a horse than from getting eaten by a shark."

I don't know where Ansel got that information, or if it's even true, but he says it with such confidence that Hayes's face relaxes slightly.

While Ansel focuses on Hayes, trying to help him onto his board, Will and I wade into the warm water. I lie belly down on my board and start to paddle out.

I know he's watching me and that makes me brave. Or stupid, depending on how you look at it, because I pick a wave that is a little bigger than I would usually ride. I'm not normally a show-off, but I want to impress him.

Will is sitting on his board, his legs dangling in the water. "That was amazing!"

I smile. He's impressed and I should leave it at that, but instead I decide to try it again. This time I paddle out a bit farther. Except I know as soon as I pop up on my board this time that it's a mistake—this wave is way more than I can handle. Fear runs up my spine. I think about bailing, but I'm already in the tube, so there's nothing to do but see how long I can hold on.

I crouch as low as I can. My thigh muscles are working overtime to keep me upright, but it's not enough—the board slips out from under my feet and I'm thrown headfirst into the water. My board clips me on the side of the head and I cry out in pain as the water closes over me. I start to panic. I break through the water but another wave crashes over me and pushes me back under. I'm flailing around, terrified, when someone grabs my arm and hauls me up.

"You're okay, Marty," Will says. "I've got you. You're okay."

I'm coughing and gasping, trying to draw air into my lungs.

Will wraps his arm securely around my shoulders. He helps me onto my board—it's still connected to my ankle with a surf leash. Once he's sure I've got a good grip, he tows me to shore.

I'm shivering as he drags the surfboard onto the sand. He kneels by my side, his blue eyes crinkled with concern. Realizing something is going on, a small crowd starts to gather around me. I hear them murmuring, wondering what happened.

Someone passes Will a T-shirt. I wince as he gently holds it against my forehead.

"I'm fine," I say, trying to sit up. "I just had the wind knocked out of me."

"Why don't you just lie still for a few more minutes?" Will says.

But I don't want to lie here with everyone staring at me. So instead of taking his advice, I push myself up.

And even though Will is right beside me, he's not quite quick enough to catch me when I pass out.

Thirteen

When I come to, Ansel is pushing his way through the crowd, his face twisted with panic. "What happened?"

"She's okay," Will says, still pressing the T-shirt to the wound on my forehead. "Head wounds bleed a lot. They always look a lot worse than they actually are."

But I must look really bad, because my brother drops to his knees in the sand beside me. He picks up my hand and squeezes. Hayes is standing just behind him, his forehead creased like an accordion.

My throat feels coated with sand and all I can taste is salt water. The sun is beating down on me, and lying on top of this hard surfboard is killing my back. But all of that is more comfortable than being watched by a bunch of random people.

"I need some water," I say. My voice cracks.

Will lets up the pressure on my forehead. Hayes holds a water bottle out to him. Ansel loops his arm around my back and helps me slowly sit up.

"Just take small sips," Will instructs, twisting the cap off the water bottle and handing it to me.

I'm too thirsty to listen, so I end up gulping the water and then spitting half of it back up when I drink it too fast.

Something wet trickles down my face. I feel like I might pass out again as Will holds the T-shirt back up to my forehead.

Is this day over yet?

"We should get you to the hospital," he says.

"I'm fine," I insist. I don't feel fine, but I really don't want to go to the hospital. I'm not sure what our medical insurance covers and I don't want my mom to have to pay for an unnecessary hospital visit. I just want to go home and pretend this whole situation never happened.

"Let's let the doctor tell us that," he says. "You okay to stand up?"

I nod.

The crowd claps as Will and Ansel work together to lift me to my feet. My face burns. I'm glad that they have their arms around me because my legs don't feel like they can support me at the moment. It's awkward walking with Will's hand pressed to my forehead, but we manage to make it to the parking lot. Ansel crouches down to slide my slippers onto my feet so I don't have to walk barefoot over the gravel.

Will settles me into the backseat of the van and then climbs in beside me.

"What about your boards?" I ask my brother as he buckles up my seat belt. We left them behind on the beach. Ansel saved up for months for his board. My throat closes.

"Hayes and I will go back and grab them," he answers. "Don't worry."

I let out a breath.

Ansel and Hayes hurry back to the beach. After they've loaded the surfboards into the back of the truck, they pile into the front and Ansel peels out of the parking lot, gravel crunching under the tires.

———

"There are a million people here," Hayes says, glancing around the packed waiting room at Maui Memorial. "This is going to take forever."

Will shoots him a dirty look. "Somewhere else you need to be?"

"You guys don't have to wait with me," I say. I wouldn't blame them if they didn't want to—they came to Maui for a vacation; it's a lot to expect for them to sit in a hospital waiting room for who knows how long.

"Yes, we do," Will answers firmly. He guides me to an orange plastic chair.

Ansel returns from checking me in. "It's going to be a while," he says.

"I could have told you that," Hayes grumbles.

We're all still in our beach attire. The orange chair is hard against my bare legs and I'm feeling itchy from the sun and sand. My head is throbbing and every time I let up pressure on the T-shirt, blood runs down my face.

Ansel checks his phone. He grimaces, and I remember that he's supposed to work this afternoon.

"Just go," I say.

He shrugs. "I'll call in sick."

"No way." I can't let him do that. He doesn't get paid when he takes a sick day.

"Someone should be with you when you get out of here," he says. "Mom's out with Auntie Kaye for the day."

"I'm fine," I say. "You heard what Will said—head wounds just bleed a lot."

"You look like something out of a horror movie," Hayes says.

"I'll stay with Marty," Will says to my brother. "We can bring her back to the hotel. We'll look after her."

If I wasn't in so much pain, I would smile. It's really sweet that Will wants to be here with me.

Ansel glances at me, uncertain. "Are you sure?"

"I'll be fine," I repeat.

"You're lucky that surfboard missed your eye," the doctor says an hour later, after he finishes stitching me up. "You'll probably have a scar, but it shouldn't be too bad." He leans forward to admire his handiwork.

I shift on the examination table, and the paper underneath me crinkles. Seven stitches, just above my left eyebrow.

"Scars are badass," Will says from his perch on the rolling stool beside the doctor. I know he's trying to cheer me up, but he's not the one who has to walk around with the memory of this day on his face forever. I may have to consider bangs.

The doctor gently tapes a large white bandage to my forehead. "Take it easy for the next few days," he says. "Tylenol if you need it. The stitches will dissolve in a week or so. No swimming."

I give him a weak smile. No need to worry about that. It will be a while before I'm brave enough to get back into the water.

I take a deep, shuddering breath. I can't stop thinking about the waves closing over my head, how quickly I could have been in real trouble if Will hadn't seen me go under.

The doctor removes his rubber gloves, rolls them into a ball, and pitches them into the garbage can like he's sinking a basket. He types something into his iPad and sends us out to reception.

In my first stroke of good luck in a while, it turns out that my dad is still paying for our medical insurance and it will cover most of the cost of this visit. Most, but not all—the bill is still three hundred dollars, an amount that makes my stomach hurt. I wonder if there will ever be a day when I don't have to worry about money.

Will calls an Uber. He asks the driver, an older woman with short white hair, to stop so he can grab some pain medication for me—my head is throbbing and the skin around my stitches feels rubbed raw. Hayes waits with me while Will runs into the pharmacy. Every time I close my eyes, he pokes me, even though I've told him repeatedly that I don't have a concussion. The Uber driver has turned the air conditioning off, but I'm still shivering in just my bathing suit and T-shirt. I'm touched when Hayes pulls a wrinkled shirt out of his bag and tucks it around me like a blanket.

"I got extra strength," Will says, climbing back into the car. He shakes out two pills and hands them to me, along with a bottle of red Gatorade. I swallow the pills as we make our way toward the Grand Palms, hoping that we don't hit any traffic.

"Thank you, by the way," I say as we leave behind the big box stores and strip malls and head toward the resort. "I don't know what would have happened if you hadn't . . ." The lump in my throat is so big, I can't even finish the sentence. It's starting to hit me, finally, that I could have drowned.

Will slides his arm around me and I lean against his shoulder. "I'm just glad you're okay," he says.

But I'm not sure how much longer that's going to hold true. Karma is not finished with me yet. I've already sent back two of the items I've stolen, but my luck still stinks. I just hope that I can send the rest back before anything worse happens.

Fourteen

Unless we're working, the staff isn't supposed to be in the guest rooms. I don't think Marielle would consider hanging out in Will's suite part of my job, so just to be on the safe side, we head into the hotel separately—Will and Hayes through the lobby, me through the service entrance.

Nalani is waiting for me just inside the door. I texted her on the way over. She's on a break, so she's in her uniform, her hair pulled back into two stubby French braids.

Her eyes widen. "Yikes, that's one big bandage."

My hand flies up to my forehead self-consciously.

"I mean . . . it's not that bad," she says as we walk

toward the elevator. She pulls me back slightly to prevent me from looking at myself in the mirrored doors.

If it's not that bad, then why won't she let me look?

The doors slide open and she ushers me into the elevator. She pushes the button for the eighth floor. I lean against the wall. My legs still feel a bit wobbly, and all I really want is to lie down and sleep the day away.

We reach Will's floor. The King Lunalilo Suite is at the end of a long hall. I haven't been in this room before, but I've heard that it has the best view of the ocean in the entire hotel.

Nalani knocks and Will answers the door right away. He's traded his beach wear for a pair of shorts and a white T-shirt with Spock on it.

"Now that you're safely delivered, I have to get back to work," she says. She gives Will the Vulcan salute and hustles back down the hall.

This suite is like something out of a magazine—if you overlook the signs of the two teenage boys staying here, that is. The high ceilings and the floor-to-ceiling windows are designed to showcase the amazing view. The furniture is simple but clearly expensive, and in the corner of the room there's a tall white sculpture that kind of looks like a giant bowling pin. I recognize it as John Koga's work, my mom's favorite Hawaiian artist. Someone has put a Red Sox ball cap on it.

Hayes wanders into the room. He's changed into a navy-blue smoking jacket, a big white *H* embroidered on the pocket, and a white captain's hat, of all things. He slips behind the built-in bar in the corner of the room and reaches into the minibar for a carton of grapefruit juice. He dumps the juice into a cut-crystal glass, then twists the cap off a tiny bottle of vodka and slops half of it into his drink.

Will shakes his head, but he doesn't say anything to his brother.

"You must be tired," he says to me. "You want to lie down in my room?"

I'd like to lie down in his room with him, but I don't think that's what he means.

"A nap is probably a good idea," I say.

"A nap is always a good idea," Hayes says.

Will continues to ignore him and leads me down the hall. We walk past a closed door that I assume belongs to Hayes. The master suite is next to it and I catch a glimpse of a huge room with a king-sized bed covered with a fluffy white duvet. Will's room is at the end of the hall.

You can learn a lot about a person from what they keep in their room. Here's what I learn about Will

Foster: he's tidy—his T-shirts and shorts are all hanging neatly in the closet. A lot of guests don't even bother unpacking; they just live out of their suitcase. He's a reader, which I already knew, but he must spend a lot of time doing it because there are several ancient sci-fi books stacked on his nightstand along with an e-reader. His lucky red plastic telescope, a moleskin notebook, and an expensive-looking silver pen are balanced on top of the books.

I wonder what he's written in that notebook.

"Sorry, housekeeping hasn't been in yet," he says when he notices me glance at the bed. He's actually done a pretty good job of making the bed—not that it's hard—but I'm impressed that he bothered. It's not something most guests do.

Will moves to the window and lowers the shade, darkening the room. I can no longer see his face, just the outline of his shape as he walks back toward me.

"Holler if you need anything." He touches my arm, his fingers as light as a butterfly on my skin, and I imagine what it would feel like to hug him. The top of my head would rest right in the hollow of his collarbone.

"Sleep well, Marty," he says. He pulls the door shut behind him.

I climb under the covers. The pillow smells like coconut, from whatever product Will uses to get his hair looking like early Elvis. I imagine him lying here, in this exact spot, staring up the ceiling. Thinking about me the way I'm thinking about him. And despite the fact that my head is throbbing, I fall asleep with a smile on my face.

Fifteen

When I wake up, it takes me a minute to figure out where I am. But then my forehead throbs and the events of this morning come rushing back to me. I sit up and turn on the lamp, spotting a bottle of water and Tylenol that someone—most likely Will—has left for me on the nightstand. Apparently I was out so hard, I didn't even hear him come into the room.

I down the Tylenol, then get out of bed. Will's also left a thick white towel and one of his T-shirts for me at the foot of the bed. I pop into the huge marble bathroom attached to his room and turn on the shower. I glance in the mirror. It's the first time I've seen myself since the accident and my stomach squirms at the sight of the stark white bandage taped to my fore-head.

Not getting the bandage wet in the shower isn't easy, but I manage. I step back into my bathing suit, then pull Will's T-shirt on. It hangs just above my knees.

Before I leave his room, I glance at his notebook on the nightstand, wondering again what he writes in it. For a moment I consider peeking inside, to see if there's anything about me in there, but the moment passes. Evidence that I'm becoming a better person with each passing day.

I hear laughter as I go down the hall. Will, Hayes, and Nalani are sitting cross-legged in a circle on the living room floor, surrounded by plates of food, having a makeshift picnic. Nalani has changed out of her housekeeping uniform and into a white dress.

I blush as Will's eyes pass over me in his T-shirt.

"I ordered your favorite," Nalani says as I sit down beside her.

"Thanks," I say. She passes me a china plate with a grilled mac-and-cheese sandwich sliced diagonally, a fat dill pickle on the side.

"A mac-and-cheese sandwich?" Hayes asks as I grab a bottle of ranch dressing from one of the trays and squirt a large blob onto my plate.

"It's a grilled cheese, but instead of just regular cheese, there's macaroni squished inside it," I say, suddenly self-conscious as the Foster brothers stare at my meal. It can be pretty messy to eat, so the last thing I want is Will watching me shovel it into my mouth. Nothing spells romance like having food all over your face.

Hayes's eyes narrow. He looks like he might have just woken up too, or maybe he's just hungover. "Is that a Hawaiian thing? Like shave ice?"

"It's a Marty thing," Nalani replies.

I hold out half of the sandwich to him. "You want to try it?"

He shakes his head. "Nope. I'm good."

"Come on," Nalani says. "Be brave."

He makes a face, but he grabs the sandwich from me and takes a small bite. "It's good," he admits.

"Wait till you try Spam musubi," I say.

"Spam, as in canned ham?" Will asks.

I nod. I'm kind of surprised he knows what it is. I can't imagine they serve it in the places he goes to. Then again, some of the best restaurants on the island have Spam on the menu.

"Is that another one of your inventions?" Hayes asks me as a piece of roast beef falls out of his sandwich and onto his bare knee.

"Spam is big in Hawaii," Nalani says. "There's a Spam festival in Waikiki every spring."

"Spam Jam," I add. I've made the pilgrimage to O'ahu for the festival a few times over the years with my brother and our friends.

"That can't be a real thing," Hayes says.

"Oh, it is." Nalani scrolls through her phone and pulls up a photo. She turns the screen to show them a picture of her holding up a doughnut covered in tiny pink chunks of Spam.

"You put it on doughnuts?" Will asks, wrinkling his nose.

"We put it on everything," I reply, but I'm distracted. Nalani's always taking photos, even when we were working together. I don't know why I didn't think of this before. It's totally possible that she took a picture when we were cleaning the room that belonged to the creepy old guy and his hot young girlfriend.

Nalani and I had just finished making the bed when the woman we'd seen sunning herself on the balcony came into the room. She was wearing a black mesh cover-up over a purple bikini, her sunglasses pushed up into her blond hair like a headband. She smelled like sunscreen.

Nalani and I might as well have been ghosts from

the way the woman's eyes slid past us as she glanced around the room.

She walked over to pick up a gold watch from the bureau and slid it around her tanned wrist.

"Did you change the sheets?" she said, fussing with the clasp on her watch.

Nalani and I exchanged a wary glance. She'd just checked in last night. If the guests were staying for an extended period, we were instructed to change the sheets every three days. Unless, of course, the guest specifically asked us to do it every day.

"Yes, ma'am," Nalani said, smiling brightly.

I was always amazed that she could keep such a straight face when she lied.

The woman didn't acknowledge that she'd heard us. Nalani gave her the finger as she left the room. She picked up a hula-girl shot glass from the nightstand, the kind that you could get for two dollars at any souvenir store in Hawaii, and took a photo of herself pretending to do a shot. Then she posted the photo on Instagram.

"Aren't you worried someone from the hotel will see that?" I asked her as I started to fold the towel swans.

"Nah," she said. "My account is private. The only person from the hotel who follows me is you."

She handed me the shot glass. Just before we left the room, I slipped it into my pocket.

I smile. That's it! The photo Nalani posted would be time-stamped. I just need to look at her feed and I'll know which of the two days is the right shift. From there, I should be able to figure out which room I took that stupid hula shot glass from.

While the three of them continue talking about Spam—Will wants to find somewhere on the island that serves Spam poke bowls—I pull my phone out of my pocket and scroll through Nalani's photos. It consists mostly of pics of whatever she had for lunch and her dog, Daisy—and, sure enough, there's one of Nalani in her uniform, her head tipped back, holding the shot glass to her mouth. The hula girl is winking at the camera. My shoulders relax.

"But why not?" Hayes says. "We're just sitting around, doing nothing. I thought you wanted to go?"

"I do, but we don't have to drop everything and go right this second," Will says. "We have plenty of time. Besides, I don't think Marty's up for it."

I look up from my phone. Somehow I managed to tune out the rest of their conversation. "Up for what?"

"Road trip to Hana," Nalani says, grabbing the last deep-fried risotto ball and popping it into her mouth.

I frown. "It's a pretty long drive. There's no way we

could make it there and back before nightfall." The road runs parallel to a cliff in some parts and there aren't any streetlights, so once the sun sets, it's almost guaranteed we'd drive over the cliff and into the ocean. Which is really not what I'm looking to do.

Hayes shrugs. "So we'll stay overnight."

"I'm in," Nalani says, which doesn't surprise me.

I open my mouth to say no—my head still hurts and Will's right, I'm not up for it—but Nalani anticipates I'm going to pull out my built-in excuse: my mother.

"Just tell her you're staying at my place," she says.

An overnighter with the Foster boys is definitely not what Marielle had in mind when she assigned me to show them around the island. This is a bad idea, but they're all looking at me expectantly and I don't want to be a wet blanket. Not when they're all so excited.

"I guess we're going to Hana," I say.

———

I borrow a pair of way-too-big board shorts from Will so I don't have to walk through the hotel in just a T-shirt. While he and Hayes throw a few things together, I tell Nalani that I'm going downstairs to grab something from my mom's office. Now that I have the exact date of our shift, I want to see if I can find the name of the person I stole the shot glass from.

"You want me to come with you?" she asks. She's lying on one of the loungers on the balcony, her face turned up to the sun.

"No. I'm fine. I'll meet you at the van."

Once I'm safely locked in my mom's office, I pull up the list of ten rooms we cleaned that day on my mom's computer. All of the rooms faced the gardens, so that doesn't narrow it down at all. However, three of the accounts had children registered in the hotel's kids club, so I can take those rooms off the list. I start googling the names of the other seven guests, to see if any photos turn up that match my memory of the older man in the bathrobe.

The fourth name I try is Dr. Stephen Markle. I find a website for a plastic surgeon in Wilmington, Delaware. Sure enough, when I click on his bio, up pops a photo of a serious-looking man in a doctor's coat. His hair is darker and fuller in this picture, but I recognize him immediately. I smile. Only one more item to go.

———

I still don't feel well enough to drive, so Nalani is behind the wheel. I'm trying not to worry about the mileage we're going to put on the van and whether Marielle will notice and question me about it.

Since my house is on the way, we decide to stop so

I can run in and grab a few things. My mom is still out, but I'm anxious as Nalani pulls the van into my driveway. I'm not embarrassed by where I live, exactly, but my house is definitely a downgrade compared to what Will and Hayes are used to.

I hear Libby meowing as I walk down the hall toward my room, and feel a stab of guilt for leaving her on her own so much. When I open the door, she tries to bolt between my legs.

"Sorry, Libs," I say, nudging her gently back inside with my foot. I close the door so she can't escape, and that's when I notice she's clawed the hell out of the wood.

"Libby, no!"

She looks up at me, all squishy gray face and wide green eyes, and the irritation drains out of me. It's not her fault she's trapped in here. I really have to find a home for her. It's not fair to keep her locked up like this.

I sigh and lean down to scratch her behind her ear. Despite my better judgment—and my brother's warnings—I've become attached to her.

I quickly change her litter and set down some fresh food and water, then shoot my brother a text asking him to check on her tonight. I don't tell him where I'm going, but he already knows I was spending the afternoon at the hotel with Will, so I'm sure he'll make the leap and assume I'm still with him. He won't be happy—no matter how well they all got along this morning, my brother definitely won't be jazzed to know I'm spending the night with Will. Even if it is totally innocent. Will said he'd book a separate hotel room for me and Nalani, so there's no need to feel awkward or weird.

It's only one night, so I don't need to pack much, just a change of clothes, some pj's, and sunscreen. I slip out of Will's shorts and pull on a pair of my own. I stuff a couple of dresses for Nalani and me into my backpack, along with some T-shirts and hoodies.

I'm about to leave the room, when I backtrack to grab one more thing. I open my closet and reach for the shoebox. After my accident this morning, I'm even more determined to send the rest of these stolen items back as soon as possible. I stick the shot glass in my backpack, promising myself that I'll mail it to Delaware when I reach Hana.

After saying goodbye to Libby, I stop in the kitchen to leave a note for my mom. I could just text her, but this way, she can't say no. I can't tell her that I'm working, because she knows my schedule, so I tell her a version of the truth: *Road trip to Hana with Nalani. Home tomorrow. Love you.*

I'm sure she will blow up my phone when she gets the note, so I turn it off. I'll deal with the fallout tomorrow.

I lock the house and walk back down the driveway.

"Everyone wants to have sex with Lara Croft," Nalani says as I slide open the van door. "So that's a boring answer."

"Fine, who would you pick?" Hayes is beside her in the passenger seat, working his way through a bag of sunflower seeds. I frown. I just know I'm going to find the shells for those seeds all over the van.

"It's a toss-up between Luke Cage or Wolverine," Nalani replies.

Hayes shakes his head. "You can't have sex with Wolverine. He'd shred you with his claws."

"They're retractable. He'd put them away after he used them to rip off my clothes," she says, laying a hand against her chest and fluttering her eyelashes at him.

Hayes almost chokes on his sunflower seeds.

"I'm not quite sure how we got here," Will says to me as I climb in beside him, slinging my bag to the floor. "But somehow the conversation has taken a turn."

Nalani glances over her shoulder at me. "We're talking about fictional characters we'd like to bang." She smiles. "I know who Marty would pick."

She starts to sing "Friend Like Me" totally off-key, and I blush hard.

"You want to have sex with the genie from *Aladdin*?" Hayes asks, like I'm some kind of deviant.

I roll my eyes. "Not the genie. Aladdin. I was ten. And I never said I wanted to have sex with him."

"That may be true, but you definitely have a type," Nalani says. "Dark hair, dark eyes."

I can feel dark-haired/dark-eyed Will looking at me.

"What about you, Will?" Nalani asks as she backs out of the driveway.

"I've never thought about it."

"Will has a thing for dark hair, too," Hayes chimes in. "Long dark hair. Like yours, Marty."

Will's face starts to go red. He clears his throat. "What is the point of this conversation, exactly?"

I turn to look out the window, hiding a smile. Something is definitely happening between us.

Hana isn't somewhere you can get in a hurry—it's a twisty stretch of narrow road through a rain forest, most of it just one lane. The speed limit is only twenty-five miles per hour. The highway is bordered by the ocean, steep cliffs, and a million bridges.

"So I know you mentioned that the road was twisty, but man, it is *really* twisty," Will says ten minutes into the journey.

"I'd like to tell you that it gets better, but I'd be lying," Nalani replies. "Hayes, I will kill you if you throw up."

I glance at Hayes. He's leaning his head against the back of the seat, his eyes closed. He does look a little green.

"Shouldn't have eaten all those sunflower seeds," he says.

"All that alcohol probably didn't help, either," Will responds.

"Maybe roll the window down." There's currently nowhere to pull over and no way to turn around, not for miles and miles anyway. It would really not be good if he threw up in the van.

What feels like ages later, the road finally widens slightly. I spot a lookout point with a coconut stand. Nalani pulls onto the shoulder of the road. "I'll get you something to drink," I say, grabbing my wallet out of my bag. "Maybe that will help settle your stomach."

"We should probably all get some air," Will says.

The coconut stand is a rustic shack built out of mismatched wood set near the edge of a cliff. A clumsily built split-rail fence is the only thing separating it from the waves crashing below. Hayes clutches his stomach as he follows Nalani over to the weathered wooden bench beside the shack.

"Aloha," the girl behind the counter says. She's wearing a red pareo, her blond hair twisted into two bear-ear buns on the top of her head.

"Four coconuts, please."

We watch as she picks up a machete and pries off the top of a green coconut, then digs a hole in the center and pops a bendy straw through the hole. She passes the first coconut to me before repeating the process for the other coconuts.

Before I can pay, Will hands her a twenty-dollar bill, depositing some of the change into the tip jar on the counter, and we carry the coconuts over to Nalani and Hayes. A breeze is blowing off the blue-green water of the Pacific Ocean.

"You look a little better," I say, giving Hayes his coconut. The color has started to return to his cheeks.

"That's because he threw up behind that eucalyptus tree over there," Nalani says.

Hayes takes a sip from his coconut and makes a yuck face. "And this just might make me heave again."

"It's an acquired taste," I say. "I promise it will make you feel better. You just have to power through it."

Hayes pulls a tiny bottle of rum out of his pocket and holds it up. "Well, if it doesn't make me feel better, this certainly will."

"Seriously?" Will says, shaking his head as his brother adds a healthy dose to his drink. Nalani holds her coconut out, but then curses, remembering that she's our driver, and pulls back before he can add any.

"Will, you really need to lighten up," Hayes says. "We're on vacation."

Will's mouth tightens.

"So what do you want to do when we get to Hana?" Nalani asks.

"What is there to do?"

"It's pretty quiet," I say. Especially at night. I assumed we would hang out in the hotel, but I should have realized that what Hayes is looking for is a party. And that's definitely not something he's going to find in Hana.

"Great," he says sullenly. "How much longer until we get there, anyway?"

"A few more hours," I say, doing my best to keep the irritation out of my voice. He seems to have forgotten that this trip was his idea in the first place.

He groans.

"There's a waterfall about an hour away that's pretty spectacular. We can stop there for a swim," Nalani says.

We walk back toward the van—some of us slightly

more steadily than others. As soon as we get close to the vehicle, I notice that the passenger door is wide open.

I pinch the bridge of my nose. "Any chance one of you left the door open?"

From their silence, I know the answer.

Nalani runs toward the van and pokes her head inside. "Everything's gone."

"Aw man," Hayes cries. "My Burberry bag! I was on a wait list for months for that bag."

I close my eyes. Maui has a lot of petty theft. Nalani and I both know this—everybody on the island knows this—and yet we didn't lock the van. We stupidly left our bags right out in the open. All someone had to do was open the door and grab the bags. Which they did.

I can't help but think that this is Karma. After all, I stole from others; it only makes sense that the universe would balance that out by having someone steal from me. I just wish that my friends hadn't been caught in the cross fire.

I have my phone and wallet on me, thank goodness, but I've lost my clothes—and the shot glass.

My legs suddenly feel weak. How am I supposed to get my luck back if I can't send that stupid shot glass back?

"They even took my sunflower seeds," Hayes says. "Who would take a half-empty bag of sunflower seeds?"

What can I say to that? I took a novelty shot glass, of all things—which just proves that I have more in common with this thief than with the Foster brothers.

"We should probably just head back to the Grand Palms." I can survive twenty-four hours in what I'm currently wearing, but I'm not sure any of us are in the road-trip mood any longer.

"Okay, this is definitely a setback," Will says. "But I think we should keep going, if you guys are up for it. We've come this far. We can pick up whatever we need when we get to Hana."

"That's easy enough for you, but Marty and I don't have a billion dollars to throw around on new stuff," Nalani says, crossing her arms.

"Nalani," I say, horrified. Sure, Will just assumed that it wouldn't be a problem to replace our stolen stuff because he comes from a place where money isn't an issue. I know she's making a not-so-subtle point about his entitlement, and she's not wrong, but I still wish she'd kept her mouth shut. Drawing attention to our financial situation is embarrassing.

"She's right. I wasn't thinking," Will says, his cheeks burning. "New stuff is on me."

I know he's trying to do the right thing, but honestly, this just makes me feel worse.

"In that case," Nalani says, smiling. "Let's keep going."

I'd really rather not. I'm upset about losing that shot glass—seriously, what am I going to do? But once again, they're all staring at me expectantly and so, once again, I give in.

Sixteen

I am in a mood.

I haven't said anything since we left the coconut stand half an hour ago. Will keeps shooting questioning glances at me, but I ignore him. All I can think about is that shot glass. And okay, it's not like it's unique—there are a million of them on the island—but I'm worried that if I buy another one and mail it off instead, it won't count. But that's pretty much my only option.

We arrive at Wailele Farm, where Twin Falls is located. I feel marginally less cranky after we buy some bottles of water and pineapple spears at the farm stand in the parking lot.

"Are you sure we're going in the right direction?"

Hayes asks as we walk across the gravel toward the jungle. We pass by houses' KEEP OUT signs to discourage tourists from wandering onto private property. "There was a waterfall back there."

"There's a better one up here," Nalani says.

Hayes lets out a heavy sigh as we walk into the jungle. It's as humid as a greenhouse. My T-shirt is already sticking to my lower back as we head down a path lined with tall green stalks of bamboo that block out most of the sun and trap in the heat. The wind blows through the bamboo cane, knocking them gently together, making a sound like wind chimes.

I slap at a mosquito on my arm. "We may regret doing this without bug spray," I say. Another thing that was in my backpack, along with my sunscreen.

"Are we there yet?" Hayes says. He's trailing behind Nalani and Will and me.

"No," Will replies, an edge to his voice. His patience is clearly running out with his brother and I can't say I blame him. Hayes seems preprogrammed to complain about everything.

Five minutes pass before he starts in again. "Why didn't anyone tell me we were going to have to hike a million miles?" he grumbles. "I would have waited for you back in the air-conditioned van."

"Hayes, you really need to lighten up," Will says, parroting his brother's words back to him. "We're on vacation."

A chunk of pineapple whizzes past Will's ear. Will laughs.

We cross over a wooden plank and trudge up a small hill. I've been to this waterfall a few times before and Nalani's right—it's worth the hike. A few minutes later we hear a rush of water as the forest parts to reveal two twin waterfalls spilling down the side of a cave that's almost hidden behind a curtain of vines. A group of hikers are sitting on slick black rocks that rim the pool of green water. A few people are swimming.

Will immediately peels off his T-shirt. He's quickly down to his black boxer shorts—his swimsuit was in his stolen bag, but apparently that's not going to stop him from getting into the water. The sight of his washboard abs, the line of dark hair that starts at his belly button and disappears under the waistband of his underwear, makes me light-headed.

Hayes and Nalani strip down, too. Like me, Nalani still has her swimsuit on underneath her clothes and her tiny yellow bikini makes Hayes's eyes bug out.

While the boys wade in the pool, yelping at the

coldness of the water, I sit down on the black rock. I tell Nalani I'll stay and guard our stuff.

"Are you sure?" she says. "You could still go in. Just don't get your bandage wet."

But I don't want to take the chance. Given how my luck has been lately, I'll probably end up with a flesh-eating infection or something.

"It's fine," I say, hoping they won't be in the water too long. The rock is not super comfortable to sit on and the mosquitos are eating me alive. I've already got two big red bites on my ankle.

Hayes screams. "Oh my god, something just brushed against my leg! Are there jellyfish in here?"

Nalani rolls her eyes. "You'd be out of your mind with pain if it was a jellyfish," she says. "There isn't anything living in here that I'm aware of."

"Well, something just touched me!"

I slap at another mosquito, watching Will float on his back. The late-afternoon sun filters through the trees, reflecting off his body. Nalani flies across the pond on the rope swing, yelling like Tarzan.

After a few minutes, Will climbs out. His under-wear sticks to his skin, not leaving a whole lot to the imagination, and I feel a blush creep over my cheeks as he sits down beside me. We don't have any towels—

also stolen!—so he shivers for a few minutes until the sun works its magic and dries him off.

"It's so beautiful here," he says. "Kind of prehistoric. Like going back in time to when dinosaurs roamed the earth."

"Maybe that's what Hayes felt in the water," I say, and Will laughs. "Actually, these falls are supposed to be an energy vortex." I'm not sure if it's myth or just good marketing, but this island supposedly has a ton of healing properties. There are a bunch of wellness retreats in Hana where tourists pay big bucks to do yoga and get massaged with crystals.

"What's an energy vortex, exactly?" he asks.

"No idea."

His bare leg brushes against mine and I definitely feel a surge of energy. It takes me back to the other night, when we were lying on the lounge. Before it collapsed.

"Do you feel any different?" he asks.

It takes me a second to realize he's asking about the vortex and not our all-too-brief physical contact.

I swallow. "Nope."

"Yeah, me either."

Will suddenly stiffens as Hayes climbs up the side of the rock, obviously intent on flinging himself from the top of the cave and into water. Apparently he didn't learn anything from his dive into the swimming pool at the mansion.

"Hayes! Are you sure that's a good idea?"

Hayes shrugs. Then he cannonballs into the water, sending up a spray that almost reaches us.

Will sighs when his brother resurfaces a few seconds later. "I promised my parents he wouldn't die on this trip, but I'm beginning to think that's one promise I won't be able to keep."

"I think it's nice that you look out for him."

"Nice," Will says, wincing. "You think I'm nice?"

"What's wrong with nice?"

"It's pretty much the kiss of death."

"What does that mean?" I ask.

"In my experience with girls, *nice* means 'Buddy, you've got no chance.'"

My heart starts to jackhammer in my chest. Is he insinuating that he's hoping to have a chance with me?

I think he is.

"Maybe you've just been talking to the wrong girls," I say.

A slow smile spreads over Will's face. Something electric passes between us and I'm positive that he's thinking about kissing me. I really wish we were alone. I feel like we could be something really great if only we had more time—and we weren't separated by thousands of miles.

A cloud passes overhead, momentarily blocking out the sun. I tell myself that not everything is a sign—sometimes a cloud is just a cloud. It's not an omen.

Will clears his throat. "You're lucky it's hot here all year long. East Coast winters are not my favorite."

"I like the idea of living somewhere where the seasons change."

"Well, then you'd definitely like Pennsylvania."

I think about Will at his Ivy League school, unhappy but trapped by obligation. Giving up his dreams to live the life his parents want for him. And my own future, living with my mom, working at the hotel. Not too long ago, that felt as comforting as a blanket. But now I'm starting to wonder if I'm actually just hiding under that blanket.

"We should probably get going," I say. "We shouldn't be driving on the twisty highway once the sun sets."

Will stands up and offers me his hand. It sends shock waves right through me, the same way it did the other night when we held hands. And if he can manage that with just a simple touch, I don't know what would happen if he did kiss me.

But I really, really want to find out.

Seventeen

The sun has completely disappeared by the time we make it to Hana. We stop at the general store to grab some supplies to replace what was stolen from the van. While Will and Hayes head for the snack aisle, I loop a wire basket over my arm and follow Nalani to the clothing section.

"Stop scratching," Nalani says, flipping through a rack of cheap T-shirts.

"I can't help it." I rub at a mosquito bite underneath my armpit—I am covered in bites and I'm itchy all over, in places I can't even reach.

Nalani holds two T-shirts up. "Which one do you want?" she says, giving me the choice between a coconut wearing lipstick or a pineapple with a lei. I reluctantly point at the pineapple, although the truth is I'd rather just keep wearing Will's shirt. But I guess at some point I'm going to need to give it back to him.

She adds a couple of pareos—purple for me, orange for her—some striped beach towels, and two pairs of neon-yellow slippers to the pile. When she starts to try on sunglasses, I wander over to the first-aid aisle to grab some calamine lotion. At this point, I will do anything to make the itching stop.

I stick a large bottle of the pink lotion into the basket, along with gauze and medical tape, in case I need to replace the bandage on my forehead. I also pick up some sunscreen, toothbrushes, and toothpaste, wondering how much this is all going to cost. Unlike Nalani, I'm not comfortable with letting Will pick up the bill, and I can't exactly put this on the hotel credit card. He's already paying for the hotel rooms. And, okay, he can afford it, but that's not the point. I don't want him to think I'm interested in his money. Especially when it's the least interesting thing about him.

I wander over to the section with tourist memorabilia and I'm relieved to find a row of the same hula-girl shot glasses as the one I stole. This one costs six dollars—which seems like a total rip-off—but it's going to have to do.

I pay for everything in my basket before setting off to find him. He's standing in front of the cooler, holding a small tray of spam musubi.

"I think I'm going to need to try this," he says.

"You haven't really lived until you do."

He gives me a look like he doesn't quite believe me, but he adds it to his basket, which is already filled with bags of chips and pretzels. We pick up a loaf of bread, a small brick of cheddar cheese, and some beef jerky. We're loading up on water when we hear Nalani and Hayes arguing from across the store.

"There's no way I'm wearing anything from this place," Hayes says. He's standing beside a shelf crammed with colorful tiki statues, holding a half-empty bottle of iced tea that I'm pretty sure he hasn't paid for yet.

Nalani snorts. "Why? You're too good for it?"

"Yes," he says. "I'll wait and get something at the resort. They have to at least have a Lacoste."

"Speaking of hotels, where are we staying?" Will asks Hayes.

"I haven't booked one yet," he replies.

I stiffen.

"Please tell me you're kidding," Nalani says.

Hayes's eyes widen at her panicked tone of voice. "I,

uh, I thought we could just pick a hotel once we were here."

"It's high season." Nalani's cheeks start to flush.

"You told me you would handle this," Will says in a I-should-have-known-better voice. He pulls out his phone and frantically starts to scroll, looking for somewhere we can spend the night. His brow furrows. "There has to be a vacancy somewhere. Every room in Hana can't be booked."

"It's . . . high . . . season," Nalani repeats slowly. "And there aren't that many hotels on this side of the island."

"Crap." Will's shoulders sag. He closes his eyes and pinches the skin at the bridge of his nose.

Hayes lets out a long, world-weary sigh. "Let's just drive back."

"We can't," I say, ignoring their confused looks as I turn around and rub my back against the glass shelf like a horse scratching itself against a post. The bite is right underneath my bathing suit strap. "I told you before we left: it's too dark to drive on the highway at night. We'd probably go right off a cliff."

"So what are we going to do then?" Hayes's voice raises an octave. His eyes dart from me to Will to Nalani.

"Well . . . I guess we'll have to sleep in the van," I say.

Hayes shakes his head. "That's not an option."

"I think it's our only option," Will says.

"It won't be so bad," I say. "At least there's enough room in there for all of us. We can put the seats down. Pretend we're camping." I used to camp with my dad. Of course, that was a long time ago. And we slept in an actual tent—although truthfully, I think the van might be more comfortable. "It's just one night."

This day has definitely played out a lot differently than I expected it to. But then, my life isn't running so smoothly lately, so I guess I shouldn't be surprised.

"We should grab some extra food and water," Nalani says. "Everything else is probably closed."

Hayes glances at his phone. "It's only eight o'clock."

She shrugs. "Hana isn't exactly a wild time, especially at night."

Hayes frowns. I guess I'm not the only one who expected this day to turn out differently.

———

Ten minutes later, after we've stocked up on snacks, we pull into the parking lot of a Thai restaurant that's already closed for the evening. Nalani parks the van behind the squat brown building so we're hidden from the street. The plan is to spend the night here and leave first thing in the morning, before the owners return and discover us camping out on their property.

"Anyone else getting a horror movie vibe?" Will asks when Nalani shuts off the headlights. A light rain has started tapping against the windshield. A motion-sensor light mounted above the back door of the restaurant shines into the van, throwing just enough light that we can make out the graffiti on the building.

"Nah. There hasn't been a murder here in years," Nalani says.

"If we were in a zombie movie, this would be the moment they'd all come stumbling out, ready to eat our brains," Hayes says.

"Well, if that happens, we can head for my house," Nalani says. "We're prepared."

"You're prepared for a zombie apocalypse?" Will replies.

She nods. "And any other kind of disaster. We have a bunker in our backyard, stocked with a million bottles of water and enough food to feed us for an entire year, in case the world goes to hell in a hand-basket."

"Could we not with the zombie talk?" I say. Zombies are pretty much the last thing I want to be thinking about while we're sitting in a dark parking lot—even if they are fictional.

"So you're totally ready if there's an earthquake or a hurricane or something?" Will asks.

"Please," she scoffs. "Any natural or unnatural disaster you can think of—nuclear war, solar flare, comet collision—we are prepared."

"She's giving you the wrong impression of her parents," I say, digging through the plastic bags to find the calamine lotion. "They're really great people." A little eccentric, sure, but well-meaning. I don't really understand why Nalani is so desperate to get away from them.

I locate the calamine lotion, but it suddenly dawns on me that I forgot to get cotton balls. I frown as I run through a list in my mind of all the things that I should have bought instead of extra beef jerky.

"Um . . . by any chance, did someone grab toilet paper?" I ask.

No one says anything.

"You're kidding, right?" Hayes says. "Please tell me you're kidding."

Nalani pops open the glove compartment. She pulls out a wad of fast-food napkins. "Jeremy must have had this van before you," she says to me. "He's always at Jack in the Box."

"Okay, but where are we supposed to go?" Hayes looks around the empty parking lot.

The rain has started in earnest, ricocheting like bullets against the van.

"Hana Bay Beach is just across the street—I'm pretty sure there's a public restroom down there," I say, twisting the cap off the calamine lotion. Nalani passes me a napkin and I douse it with the pink liquid, then dab the napkin against a row of bites on my left arm.

"It's probably locked for the night." Nalani gestures toward the jungle, about twenty yards away. "Just go behind those trees."

"You mean the trees where the escaped convict is hiding, waiting to murder me? Those trees?" Hayes says.

She nods. "Yup, those are the ones."

"Come on," Will says. "I'll go with you."

Nalani turns on the headlights so they can navigate through the dark.

"They're going to come back, right?" I say as they disappear into the bushes. "I wouldn't want to have to explain to Marielle that I lost them."

"Right. I keep forgetting that this is your job," she says.

"Me too." It doesn't feel like a job anymore. If I'm honest, it never did.

I prop my foot against the back of the passenger seat so I can apply lotion to the bites on my ankles.

"Need some help?" Nalani asks.

I nod. "I definitely do."

She climbs into the backseat. I wipe my fingers on the napkin and then shed my shirt, turning away from her so she has access to my back.

"Yikes, they really got you," she says. "You have, like, twenty bites."

I scowl. "How am I the only one who was bitten?"

"Your bad luck, I guess," she says.

My bad luck. That's what it all keeps coming back to.

"Nalani?" I ask as she dabs the lotion on so softly, I can barely feel it.

"Yeah."

I chew my lip. "I stole some stuff when we were working together."

"Like the chocolate macadamia nuts?" she says. "Because honestly, I think of those as a job perk."

"No. Like . . . from the guests."

Nalani's hand stills. "Oh."

My cheeks are hot. I'm glad I can't see her face, because I don't think I'd have the courage to tell her this otherwise. I take a deep breath. "It was stupid. And ever since I took that stuff, it's like I've been cursed," I say. "I've been sending the stuff back, but so far it doesn't seem to have made any difference."

"Marty, a few mosquito bites doesn't mean you're cursed," she says.

"What about what happened this morning? I almost drowned."

"That was an accident."

It wasn't an accident. It was Karma.

"What about all the good things that have happened over the past few months?" Nalani applies some lotion to a ring of bites on my lower back. "You were promoted to the front desk."

"I know you think it's better than working in housekeeping, but trust me, nightshift is no fun."

"There's no way that it's worse than cleaning toilets," she says. "And how do you explain getting paid to show rich tourists around the island, then?"

Nalani and I see things so differently. Sure, getting to spend time with Will has been amazing, but it would have been so much better if the only thing I felt for him was friendship. I'm having all these feelings for someone who'll be leaving at the end of the summer.

"Anyway, you're sending the stuff back," she says. "That has to count for something."

I sure as hell hope so.

After Nalani finishes with the mosquito bites, she digs in the grocery bag while I slip my shirt back on.

"So, I was thinking we should start our trip in San Francisco," she says, fishing out a granola bar. "I found a hostel that's, like, thirty bucks a night, right near Fisherman's Wharf. We could stay there for a few nights, then make our way down to San Diego."

Nalani rips open the granola bar wrapper with her teeth. She's about to take a bite when she catches the look on my face. Her eyes widen. "What's the matter?"

I swallow. I really hope she doesn't hate me for this. "I can't go with you."

"What do you mean?"

"I just . . . It's not a good time. I can't leave my mom alone." It's the truth, but it's only part of it. I'm just not brave enough to take the leap. Life is changing . . . faster than I can handle it. But I don't know how to make Nalani understand why I've decided to stay here instead of heading out on an epic adventure with her, when I don't fully understand it myself.

"Have you told your mom you're staying?" she asks.

I shake my head. I haven't talked to her about it because I don't want her to try to change my mind. I know she'd tell me to go. But I also know she needs me. Even if she wouldn't admit it.

"I'm really sorry," I say.

Nalani sighs. "This trip is definitely not going to be the same without you."

"You're not mad?"

"I'm not mad." She puts her arm around me and I lay my head on her shoulder. Relief courses through me.

"Why do you always expect the worst from people?" she asks.

I never used to. But when the person you believe will always be around, no matter what, leaves without a backward glance, it's difficult to trust anyone. Even if that person is your best friend.

Eighteen

I t smells like cat food." Hayes tries to hand the spam musubi back to Will. "I'm going to stick with pretzels."

"Just try it," Will says wearily. His hair has been flattened by his run through the rain, which hasn't let up in the past hour. We've been locked in the van, and our nerves are all starting to wear thin.

Hayes grimaces, but to my surprise, he decides to be adventurous. He takes a small bite of the sushi. After chewing for a minute, he shrugs. "If you can get past the smell, it tastes kind of like ham."

"That's because it is ham," Will says. "Sort of."

After we finish our dinner, Nalani tears open a box of animal crackers and passes a handful over the seat to me. She's sitting in front of Will and me, and Hayes is in front of her, in the passenger seat, his feet resting on the dash.

Now that my mosquito bites have calmed down, my head is starting to hurt again. I lightly touch the bandage on my forehead, feeling the bump of stitches underneath.

"You okay?" Will asks. Even though there's plenty of space for the both of us back here, he's close enough that his shoulder keeps brushing against mine. I'm pretty sure it's intentional. It sends electric shocks through me every time.

"I've felt better," I admit.

"I know what will help." Hayes leans down and searches for something underneath his seat. He holds up a bottle of tequila, a sly grin crossing his face.

Will stiffens. "Where did you get that?"

"I never reveal my sources," he says, but I notice Nalani's cheeks redden. "We're just lucky the thieves didn't find it. Otherwise we'd be facing a very sober evening."

"Put it away, Hayes," Will says.

Hayes slowly twists off the cap and takes a long, deliberate swig from the bottle, his eyes never leaving Will's.

Will throws his hands in the air. "Okay, fine. You

know what? Do what you want. I'm done worrying about it."

Hayes snorts. "You don't need to worry about me. Worry about yourself."

Will's eyes narrow. "What's that supposed to mean?"

There's not enough room in this van for all the tension. I'm glad that Hayes is just out of Will's reach— from the waves of anger radiating off Will right now, I wouldn't put it past him to grab his brother and give him a solid shake.

"Hey, there's a really great shave ice place we should hit on the way home tomorrow," I say. It's a super-lame, super-transparent attempt to divert their attention and diffuse some of the strain, and of course it doesn't work. Neither of them care about shave ice right now—they're too busy staring daggers at each other.

"Just keep doing whatever Dad tells you to do," Hayes says. "Then you don't need to think for yourself."

Beside me, Will goes very still. "At least I don't use alcohol to try to get his attention," he says. "How's that working out for you, by the way?"

Hayes's fingers tighten on the bottle of tequila. He throws open the door and steps out of the van. I don't know where he thinks he's going—it's dark and there's nothing but rain out there—but he slams the door. The windows are so steamed up, I can't see where he runs off to.

Will swears under his breath, but he doesn't make a move to go after his brother.

"You're not going to go check on him?" Nalani asks.

"Nope," he says. "I'm tired of his attitude. He'll come back once he's cooled off."

Nalani and I exchange a glance. I'm not sure how wise it is to let Hayes stumble around this time of night, especially if he starts drinking in earnest. He could easily get lost or hurt.

Nalani must feel bad about supplying him with the tequila, because she volunteers to go find him.

"Sorry," Will says to me after she leaves the van. He sighs and rubs a hand down his face. "I just don't know what else to do."

"Maybe you should tell your parents," I say. This seems like too big of a problem for him to try to handle on his own. Hayes clearly needs help.

"If my dad finds out he's been drinking again, they'll take him out of school." Will picks up one of the beach towels and rubs the condensation off the window, creating a porthole so we can see outside.

"Maybe that's what he needs," I say.

Will shakes his head. "He loves that school. He's already upset about leaving his friends behind this summer to come here with me. I can't imagine he'd take leaving them behind indefinitely very well—especially if I'm the one who rats him out. It would just push him over the edge." He's silent for a minute. "I keep hoping he'll just stop."

I'm not so sure that Hayes can just stop. There hasn't been one day that I've spent with them that he hasn't been drinking.

"What he said about me . . . ," Will says, staring out the window.

"He was just mad." Siblings always know just where to hit that will hurt the most.

He frowns. "But he's not wrong. I do everything my parents ask of me because it's easier than fighting with them. And because I feel guilty." He leans his head back against the seat. "How about your parents? How did they take it when you said you weren't going to college?"

"My mom wasn't happy about it at first," I say. "But she eventually came around once I told her that I am planning to go eventually."

Of course, that was when she thought I was taking a year off to travel. I'm not sure how she's going to feel when she finds out I'm staying home.

"But you still did it anyway." I can tell that Will thinks that rebelling against my parents makes me brave, when really, the only reason I'm in this position is because I'm afraid.

I really want to be the girl he sees. Not the one who is too scared to take a chance.

So I reach for his hand. I thread my fingers through his and tug him gently toward me, until he is barely a breath away. His lips curve into a surprised smile as he closes the distance between us and kisses me. He pulls me onto his lap and I entwine my fingers in his hair. I ignore the distant warning bell as his lips explore my neck. I know these few weeks are all that we have and that I'm bound to have my heart broken.

I know this, but I can't stop kissing him.

It might be ten minutes or two hours or an entire day later when I hear Nalani calling my name. I scramble off Will. I pull down my T-shirt and he smooths a hand over his hair, which is silly because there's no way to hide what we've been up to.

"A little help!" Nalani yells from just outside the van.

Will climbs over the seat and slides open the door. Nalani is holding on to Hayes, almost buckling under the weight of trying to keep him upright. Both of them are soaked to the skin from the rain. Hayes's legs are about as stable as seaweed. His arm is slung around her shoulders and his head is rolling loosely around on his neck, like he can't hold it up.

Will jumps out of the van and grabs his brother's waist.

"Didn't you guys hear me yelling?" she says as he lowers Hayes onto the bench seat. He lays him on his side, then gives him a solid shake to try to rouse him.

Hayes slaps Will's hand away. "What are you doing?" His voice is slurred.

"Making sure you don't die, you idiot," Will replies. His face is stony, but I can see the fear in his eyes.

"He was down at the beach," Nalani says. "By the time I found him, he'd already downed half the bottle."

Hayes's eyes drift closed and Will shakes his shoulder again.

"Stop," he mumbles.

"Should we take him to the doctor?" I say. There's a clinic in Hana, and I just hope it's open this late, because the hospital is all the way on the other side of the island.

Will shakes his head. "I've been here with him before. He just needs to sleep it off," he says. We help him prop Hayes up so Will can peel off his wet clothes. When Hayes is down to his underwear, Will guides him back down to the seat, positioning him so he's on his side, and covers him with a beach towel.

"Do you mind if I take the backseat?" Will asks us. "I'm going to stay up and watch him."

"Why don't we take shifts?" It doesn't seem fair that he has to stay awake all night.

He shakes his head. "He's my brother. I need to do it."

So Nalani and I take the front seats, reclining them all the way back until we're staring up at the roof of the van. The rain is still pounding. I don't know how I'll be able to sleep through it, but I guess I'm more tired than I thought, because as soon as I close my eyes, I'm out.

————

Sometime in the night the rain finally stopped. The sky has just started to brighten when I wake up. I'm stiff from sleeping in an awkward position and I'm freezing—beach towels don't exactly make great blankets.

Nalani is softly snoring in the driver's seat beside me. I sit up and twist around to look for Will. He gives me a small smile. Even from across the van, I can see those dark circles under his eyes.

"Did you get any sleep?" I ask him.

He shrugs.

"How is Hayes?"

"He hasn't moved," he says. "He's going to feel pretty crappy when he wakes up. Which is exactly what he deserves."

My mouth is dry and I'm sure my breath smells like death. I quietly dig in the bags for my toothbrush and toothpaste.

"I need some air," I say.

"I could use a walk."

Hayes and Nalani continue to sleep as Will climbs across the seat. We slide out of the van and walk across the parking lot. The air is cool and birds are chirping. The sun is just beginning to rise and the sky is a rose-gold pink. Will reaches for my hand as we cross the street. The feel of his palm against mine sets my heart racing.

We stop at the public restroom. Luckily, it's open. I go in first. It smells so awful, I have to hold my breath while I quickly pee and brush my teeth at the tiny, chipped porcelain sink. But I feel a lot better when I come out. Will asks to borrow my toothpaste, and I wait for him while he takes his turn in the bathroom.

We kick off our slippers, abandoning them as soon as we hit the sand. The tide is on its way out, leaving a flat stretch of black sand that's wet and cold on our bare feet. We stop when we get to the edge of the water, listening to the waves roll out.

"I don't think I'll ever get used to how beautiful it is here," Will says. He's staring out at the ocean, his hands shoved in his pockets. I sneak a look at him, studying the sharp line of his nose, the curve of his lips, his thick dark hair rustling in the breeze, and a pit forms in my stomach.

I'm falling hard for him. Will Foster has already made a mark on me that I'm scared won't ever be erased. When he leaves, I'm afraid he'll take my heart with him.

He moves behind me and wraps his arms around me, and I want this moment to go on forever. And when he plants kisses on my neck that makes me shake all over, I try to just enjoy it and not think about what will happen when he's no longer here.

"I'm going to tell my dad that I don't want to go to Wharton," Will says. "I've been thinking about it all night."

I lean back, my head resting against his shoulder. "That's great." I'm happy that he's taking charge of his own life, that he's decided to live his for himself, not for his parents.

Unlike me. Staying on the island for my mom.

It's not the same thing, I think. My mom isn't forcing me to do something I don't want to do. She doesn't even know that I'm doing it.

"Maybe I'll do some traveling," he says. "Backpack across the country."

"Backpack, as in stay in hostels?" I say, and I can't help smiling. "You know they don't have swim-up bars?"

His arms tighten around me. "It would be an adventure. And, hey, I've slept in worse places. I mean, a hostel has to be more comfortable than sleeping in a van." He kisses my neck and I shiver. "And maybe you could meet up with me."

My smile falters. It sounds great, but once Will leaves this island, he'll go back to his real life. Staying in hostels is not going to be his reality—and neither am I. Pretty soon I'll become a story, a girl he once met on vacation, and all these feelings will fade to a dream. For him, anyway.

I loosen myself from his arms. "I'm staying here, remember?"

"You'll have an entire year off," he says, drawing me back. "Just say you'll think about it."

So I tell him I will, but I don't really believe it'll happen.

Nineteen

We leave Hana just after sunrise. Hayes is incredibly hungover and it takes us longer to get back to Wailea than it normally would, because we have to pull over several times so he can throw up.

When we finally get to the Grand Palms, Hayes slides out of the passenger seat and walks off without a word.

"So that was fun," Will says, watching him go. "Sorry, again, about my brother."

"You don't need to apologize for him," I reply.

He gives me a small smile. He leans over and kisses me. I flush, feeling Nalani's eyes on us in the rearview mirror.

I'm still flushing as we climb out of the backseat and I get into the front with her.

"Are you sure you know what you're doing, Marty?" Nalani says as Will disappears into the lobby. "No tourist is worth the heartbreak, no matter how cute he is."

I glance out the window so she can't see my face. I've been telling myself the same thing, but hearing the words come out of her mouth just reaffirms the impossibility of the whole situation.

"It's not a big deal," I say. But I don't sound convincing.

We arrive at her house. Her mom is a reclaimed junk artist and their yard is littered with metal sea creatures—turtles, dolphins, a six-foot-tall mermaid. Her stepdad, Dave, is sitting on the front porch, rubbing their dog, Daisy's, belly.

Nalani puts the van in park. "You want to come in?"

It's been ages since we've hung out, just the two of us, but I'm exhausted and I just want to sleep in my own bed.

"I should probably get home."

"Are you sure you're well enough to drive?" she asks.

"I'll be fine. It's only a few blocks."

I hear Mom and Ansel arguing as soon as I pull into

our driveway. The front door flies open and Ansel storms out, his face a mask of anger.

"Run while you can," he says. "She's on a rampage."

He gets into his truck and takes off in a cloud of exhaust. I want so badly for him to take me with him, wherever it is he's going, but it's too late. My mom's standing in the doorway, her arms crossed. I get out of the van and walk toward her, feeling myself shrink under her angry glare.

"Why didn't you tell me you were in an accident?"

My fingers touch the bandage on my forehead. "I didn't want to worry you."

She shakes her head. "I have told you both, time and again, that surfing is dangerous," she says. "And you think it's okay to disappear all night?"

"Mom. I'm fine," I say. "And I didn't disappear all night. I left you a note."

"And why didn't you answer my texts?"

"My phone was off."

She takes a deep breath. I guess fighting with my brother must have worn her down because she just shakes her head again, like she doesn't have any energy left to deal with me. For a moment I feel sorry for her—until I get down to my room and see that my door is wide open.

Libby is nowhere to be found.

I run back up the stairs and into the kitchen, where my mom is calmly loading the dishwasher. This must be where her battle with Ansel broke out, because it looks like he left without finishing his blueberry pancakes.

"Where's Libby?"

"If you mean the cat you were hiding in your room, I took it to the shelter last night," my mom says. She rinses off a plate and sticks it in the lower rack of the dishwasher, like it's totally normal to just get rid of her daughter's cat with no fair warning.

And, okay, I know it was wrong to hide Libby from her, but this is exactly why I did it. She's so rigid, so unbending. I'm tired of doing things her way. All these months of holding in my feelings, of tiptoeing around her, and she can't give me this one thing.

"How could you do that?" I yell.

My mom's spine straightens. "Marty, I told you— no pets."

My chest is heaving. I'm going to cry if I stand here, and I don't want to cry. Libby was taken to the shelter hours ago—she could have been adopted by someone else by now. Or worse. "If anything happens to her, I will never forgive you."

And I'll never forgive myself.

Libby's small gray face peeks out at me from behind the cage. I poke my fingers through the metal bars and she nuzzles her head against them. Her fur is soft and warm. This is all my fault. I should have found a real home for her.

After I finish buying her back from the shelter, I take her out to the van in her carrier. I can't bring her to my house, obviously—my mom would only make me take her back here.

I sit in the parking lot, trying to figure out what to do. I want to select the family she ends up with, but that might take a while. Benjie already said he couldn't take her. Nalani's allergic to cats, so she's out.

I bite my lip and shoot a text to Will. I know it's a big ask, but he's the only person who might be able take her temporarily. When he responds right away, telling me to bring her over, I relax a little.

Fifteen minutes later Will answers his door in jogging pants and a T-shirt. My heart turns over as he blinks sleepily at me.

I wince. "I woke you up." It should have occurred to me that he'd be sleeping—he didn't get much rest last night.

"Don't worry about it." He leans forward and kisses me, then bends down to look through the cat carrier at Libby.

"I really appreciate this," I say. "It's just for a day or two, until I find a permanent home for her." He straightens and I hand him the cat carrier. Our fingers brush and I feel that touch vibrate through my body.

"No problem," he says, smiling. "I love cats."

"How's Hayes?"

"Sleeping it off," he says. "I think he's going to be out of action for a while." He sets Libby's carrier on the ground and pulls me toward him, his arms snaking around my waist. "Can you stay for a bit?"

It's really hard to say no when he's nuzzling his nose against my neck, but I have to send the shot glass back. Besides, he needs to get some sleep and I can't guarantee that he'll get any if I stay.

"I'd better not." I disentangle myself before I change my mind. "I'll see you tonight?" I'm taking him to a coffee shop in Lahaina, just the two of us, after I go home and get some sleep.

"Tonight," he says.

———

Besides the cost of mailing the shot glass, I have to buy a box and some bubble wrap so it doesn't break as it

Destination weddings were a huge business on Maui. The Grand Palms hosted weddings in its on-site chapel a few times a week. The hotel even had a full-time wedding coordinator.

While Nalani pretended to throw the bouquet, I finished making the bed. I started straightening the garbage on the top of the desk—receipts, loose change—organizing it into neat piles. Inside a small plastic bag was a blue leather luggage tag in the shape of a surfboard, Maui written on it in neon-yellow letters. Goosebumps broke out on my arms. My dad had a luggage tag similar to this one—so I guess that's why I took it. Not because I was punishing the people staying in this room, but because it reminded me of him.

I close my eyes. That was the night that we went to the bonfire, when my mom caught me and had me reassigned to the front desk. Now that I remembered the date, it shouldn't be too hard to find out what weddings were held that week. Now it's just a matter of getting the happy couple's names and I can send the last item on its way.

I let out a long, slow breath. I'm finally going to get my luck back.

makes its way to Delaware. Altogether, the shot glass costs me twenty dollars to send back to the good doctor.

By the time I get home, my mom has already left for work. She's set a plate of brownies on the counter, along with a note that I don't bother reading. Nice try, but I'm still mad at her. She can't fix this situation with baked goods.

I go to my room and pull out the shoebox. There's only one item left—the luggage tag.

"You have to come tonight," Nalani said, dumping an armful of towels into the laundry bag attached to her housekeeping cart. She'd been trying to convince me to go to the bonfire with her for the past half hour. "You can't avoid Kahale forever."

"I'm not trying to avoid him," I said. But I totally was. It had only been a few weeks since prom and I did not feel ready to see him. I'm not sure I would ever be ready. The shock of it all had worn off, but I still hadn't gotten past the hurt and humiliation yet.

I started to pull the sheets off the bed.

"Hey, look at this." Nalani pulled out a long white veil hanging in the closet and placed it on her head. She grabbed a vase of fresh plumeria flowers off the bureau and held them in front of her. "How do I look?"

"Weird."

Twenty

After I get a few hours of sleep, I go back to the hotel to pick Will up. We drive toward Lahaina with the windows down, Will's arm resting on the windowsill. Now that he's made the decision not to go to business school, he seems more relaxed. The world is an open road for him, and he can go anywhere he likes.

And maybe he's not the only one.

Ever since my fight with my mom this morning, I've been thinking about following through with my original plans to travel with Nalani. Ansel is right: I can't live my life for my mom. And if I stay on Maui, I'm just running in place, destined to go nowhere. My life will never be any different if I don't suck up the courage and take a chance. And while the idea of leaving Maui is scary, maybe that's exactly why I need to do it.

I have just enough money saved to cover a few months of travel, if I'm careful. If I had to, I could always get a job. I know Nalani will be thrilled that I've changed my mind about going with her.

So before I can talk myself out of it, I tell Will about my change in plans. "Who knows? Maybe we can meet up after all," I say.

He twists in his seat to look at me, a smile spreading across his face. "Are you serious?"

I nod, laughing when he leans out the window and howls like a wolf.

For the rest of the ride, we talk about all the places we'd like to visit—the Grand Canyon, Redwood Forest, Joshua Tree. I can't stop smiling.

I find rock star parking right on Front Street. We get out of the van and walk along the boardwalk, past tourist shops and restaurants. When we pass Ululani's, one of the most popular shave ice places on Maui, Will changes his mind about coffee.

"Maybe we should go here instead," he says as a man with a purple-and-red shave ice the size of a softball wanders past us.

He doesn't need to convince me—I'm always in the

mood for shave ice. And when he tells me he's never tried it, I grab his arm and pull him into line.

Will studies all the different choices listed on the menu. "I'm thinking the Hawaiian Rainbow," he says. It's a safe bet, a combination of strawberry, pineapple, and vanilla. "What are you going to have?"

I always order the same thing. "Lychee and sour apple with a snow cap."

"What's a snow cap?"

"It's basically condensed milk poured over the top," I say.

"Okay, you've talked me into it."

We're almost at the front of the line when his phone beeps. He glances at it and stiffens. All the color leaves his face.

"It's my brother," he says. "I have to get back to the hotel. My parents are here."

———

Will's quiet on the ride back to the Grand Palms. All the excitement has leaked out of him. No more talk of our trip, just Will tapping his fingers against his thigh while I drive, and me trying to think of something to say to break the tension that's suddenly enveloped us like a fog.

I pull into the hotel parking lot. I wonder what it means for him that his parents have shown up, unannounced. He's reacting like it's the worst news ever. As far as I know, he hasn't told them that he's not going to school yet, so this is probably just nerves.

"My dad's allergic to cats," he says. His voice is stiff.

I swallow. "Oh. Um, okay. I'll come up and grab Libby."

I really don't want to go upstairs with him and meet his parents—I'm scared of them by default—and from his closed-off body language, I don't think it's what Will wants either, but I have to get Libby.

Will stuffs his hands into his pockets as we walk through the hotel. A truck could drive through the space between us. I can't believe just a half an hour ago we were excitedly talking about all the places we'd go and now it's like I'm walking beside a stranger. I know this doesn't really have anything to do with me, but it's hard not to take his mood personally.

He takes a deep breath before unlocking the door to his suite. Maybe he was hoping Hayes was just playing a prank on him, because his shoulders slump when he sees a brass luggage cart sitting in the hall, piled high with expensive suitcases.

"William? Is that you?" a man with a distinct East

Coast accent calls from the other room, followed by a sneeze. A few seconds later Will's dad rounds the corner, Libby trotting behind him.

"William, why is there a cat in our suite?" his dad says. He's the grown-up version of Will, dressed in a light-blue golf shirt and Bermuda shorts that show off legs that clearly haven't seen the sun in a while. He's holding a Kleenex to his nose.

"Hi, Dad. What are you doing here?" Will asks.

"Your mother and I thought we'd surprise you." He lowers the Kleenex and smiles at me, but it feels more practiced than sincere.

"Hello. I'm Richard Foster," he says. His eyes don't leave my face, but I can feel him taking in my cutoff shorts and plain T-shirt, my hair pulled into a messy topknot.

My cheeks are on fire. I can only imagine what he's thinking right now—his son brought some random girl up to his hotel room.

"Hi, Mr. Foster," I say, holding out my hand to shake his. "I'm Marty."

I can feel the stress radiating off Will in waves. "Where's Mom?"

"Downstairs having tea with the Gundlesons," Mr. Foster says. "And you're avoiding my question. Why is there a cat here?"

"Right. Well . . ." Will rubs the back of his neck.

"He was doing me a favor, sir," I say, leaning down to grab Libby. "I asked him to watch her for a few days until I could find a permanent home for her. But I've found one—yay!—so I'm actually just here to pick her up."

From the way Will's dad is studying me, it's clear he doesn't buy it. He's not stupid—he knows there's more to our story than a stray cat. But he doesn't ask any follow-up questions, which is good because I don't know how well that lie would hold up under cross-examination.

"Marty works here at the Grand Palms," Will says, and I die a little. It's not much of an explanation—it certainly doesn't explain why I've left the cat with him—but even worse, with that one sentence, Will has put a gulf between us. He didn't tell his dad that we're dating—he told him that I'm the help.

"I'll just go grab the carrier," I say, feeling humiliated. I want to get out of here as quickly as possible. I can hear Mr. Foster's angry whispers as I walk down the hall with Libby tucked under my arm. I scan the main room but I don't see the carrier, so Will must have left it in his bedroom. I debate the propriety of going in to grab it, but at this point, I just want to get out of here.

The carrier is next to Will's bed. Libby gives a mournful meow as I put her inside the carrier. I grab a tote bag filled with her food, but I don't bother taking her litter box—let Will deal with that—and hurry out of his room.

When I get back to the entryway, Will's face is red and he doesn't look me in the eye. My heart sinks right down to my toes. His dad must have said something to him about me, and whatever it was, his words have hit their mark.

"Lovely to meet you, Marcy," Mr. Foster says.

I wait for Will to correct him, and when he doesn't, I say, "Nice to meet you, too."

I finally catch Will's eye, then immediately wish I hadn't. His face is blank, whatever emotions he's feeling hidden where I can't read them.

I swallow, my mouth suddenly dry. I leave the room without another word, trying not to mind that he didn't even say goodbye.

Twenty-one

I've been sitting in the hotel van for the past twenty minutes, Libby purring on my lap. Her head is resting on my leg, her eyes closed in contentment as I stroke her gray fur, and I almost can't take it. My chest hitches. Not being able to keep her is the worst. I can't bear the idea of taking her back to the shelter, but I don't know what else to do with her.

Marielle left me a message, letting me know that Will's parents have unexpectedly arrived and I'm no longer needed as a tour guide. I'm back on the front desk and she's expecting me to work tomorrow night.

My phone beeps again. I'm hoping it's Will, but it's my brother, asking me to meet him at Leoda's, a pie shop not too far from the golf course where he works.

I'm not in the mood, but when I tell him that, he says he won't take no for an answer, and so I put Libby back into her carrier and start the van.

Half an hour later, I pull off Honoapi'ilani Highway and into Leoda's parking lot. I can't leave Libby in the van—it's way too hot—so I loop her carrier over my arm, hoping that the staff will think it's my purse.

Ansel's at one of the high-top tables across from the counter. I place Libby's carrier underneath the table, then sit on the stool beside him.

He raises an eyebrow. "They're going to kick us out."

"Maybe no one will notice," I say, just as Libby lets out a loud meow. Fortunately, the woman behind the counter doesn't seem to have heard.

Ansel's knee is bouncing up and down. He digs his fork into his half-eaten piece of banana cream pie and shovels it into his mouth. He ordered pie for me—macadamia chocolate praline—but there's another slice on the table as well. Olowalu lime. My dad's favorite.

My entire body tenses. "Ansel."

He doesn't look at me, but his face reddens.

I poke his shoulder. He swallows the pie and finally meets my eyes.

"If I told you he was here, you wouldn't have come," he says.

My entire body goes cold. I glance around and spot my dad at a table on the other side of the restaurant, where he's obviously been watching us. Our eyes lock and he smiles tentatively at me, like that's going to take the sting out of being tricked into seeing him.

"You're an asshole," I say to Ansel as I slide off the stool. I snatch up Libby's carrier, feeling stupid that I didn't catch on when he suggested we meet here, at my dad's favorite pie place.

I really hate my brother right now.

"Come on. Don't go," Ansel says, grabbing my arm. "You haven't taken any of his calls. What else was he supposed to do?"

I shake him off. "Not leaving in the first place would have been nice." My voice is loud and I can feel the eyes of the other diners on me, but I don't care. I don't care about anything but getting out of here before I completely lose my shit, but it's too late, because now my dad is standing in front of me and I'm going to have to deal with this.

Six months. I haven't seen him in six months, but he hasn't changed. He still looks the same, in his khaki shorts and his washed-out T-shirt, three days' worth of beard on his face because he's too lazy to shave. But this is a trick too, because he's not the same. This person standing in front of me is not my dad. The dad who took me camping, who spent hours searching for sea turtles, who taught me to drive—that's my dad. And he never would have left.

"Marty," he says, taking a step closer to me. "Please."

I shake my head and push past him. I am going to cry and I don't want to do it front of him. I don't want him to think that I'm weakening.

"You can't ignore me forever," he says, following me outside.

Oh yeah? Watch me.

He grimaces. "I know you're angry—and you have every right to be—but I just want the chance to explain."

I throw open the passenger door of the van and place Libby on the seat. My legs are shaking as I walk to the driver's side. This time he doesn't follow me. He sighs and runs a hand through his hair, the same dark red as my brother's, as I climb into the van.

"You can't run away from your problems, honey," he calls as I back the van out of the parking spot. "Take it from me."

———

I'm on autopilot. The texts are rolling in and I know they're from my brother and/or my dad, but I ignore them. There's nothing either of them can say that I want to hear. I can't believe my brother would do that to me, knowing how I felt about my dad.

I don't know where else to go, so I go home, hoping that Ansel isn't behind me. My stomach is in knots and I'm still shaking when I pull the van into our driveway. Everything is a mess and I don't know how to make anything better. I don't even know what better looks like.

Libby gazes up at me through the mesh of her carrier. I unzip the carrier door and pull her out, settling her on my lap. She immediately starts to purr.

Mrs. Bautista, our next-door neighbor, comes out the front door of her seashell-pink house, carrying a watering can. I watch her water her hanging baskets. Mrs. B. is a retired music teacher and she's lived beside us for as long as I can remember. After my dad left, she came by our house every day for weeks, bringing homemade banana bread or a casserole. Checking in on us, the same way we checked in on her when her husband, Barry, died last year.

Libby needs a permanent home and if I can't give her that, then Mrs. B.'s house is the next best thing. I know she would love her as much as I do. I just hope she'll take her.

I take a deep breath and quickly wipe away my

tears. I climb out of the van and walk across the lawn, Libby in my arms.

"Marty." Mrs. B. pushes up the brim of her floppy yellow sunhat. Her entire face lights up when she smiles. "I haven't seen you in a while. How are you, love?"

"Hi, Mrs. B."

"Now, who might this be?" She takes off her floral gardening gloves and stuffs them into the pocket of her salmon-colored capri pants, then reaches out to stroke Libby's back. "Aren't you sweet?" she says. "I didn't know you had a cat."

"We don't," I say. "I'm actually looking for a home for her."

Mrs. B. glances at me.

"I see," she says. "Well, to be honest, honey, I swore I wasn't going to get another cat after my Henry died . . ."

But I can tell from the way she smiles at Libby that she's already been won over. Mrs. B. sets her watering can on the ground and reaches for her. I pass Libby over and she nestles into the crook of Mrs. B.'s arm, like she was always meant to be there.

"She's adorable," Mrs. B. says. "Thank you."

I nod. My throat feels thick. I reach out and scratch Libby one more time behind the ears. Tears are starting to push against my eyes again.

Mrs. B. rests her hand on my arm. "Thank you, Marty, for trusting me with her," she says. "You come back and see us anytime you like, all right?"

I admit, it does make it sting slightly less that Libby is right next door, where I can see her whenever I want.

"Thanks, Mrs. B.," I say. "Bye, Libby."

I walk back toward my house. Letting Libby go is the right thing to do. But that doesn't mean it doesn't hurt.

———

I haven't heard anything from Will since yesterday. I've texted him a few times and now I'm angry—at him because he hasn't responded and at me for trusting him in the first place. I'm sure he's busy with his parents, but he could have at least taken two seconds to text me back.

I'm beginning to think I was wrong about him. That all I was—all I was ever going to be—was a diversion from his real life. And now that his real life has come knocking, he's no longer interested in me.

It feels like rejection, like catching Kahale in the limo all over again. But I still check my phone every few minutes, hoping I'm wrong.

"You're sure you took it the night of the bonfire?" Nalani asks. She's leaning on the front desk, trying to help me find the owner of the luggage tag. She's off tonight, but I'm glad she's keeping me company, at least until Katherine, the girl I'm working this shift with returns from her break.

I sigh and put my head down on the desk. "Yes."

I've combed through the guest records for the rooms we cleaned on that date, but I haven't turned up anything that suggests the owners of the room were getting married. No complimentary champagne, no chocolate-covered strawberries or rose petals on the bed.

Nothing.

"Maybe you should check Jack's files," she says.

Jack is the hotel's wedding planner. He keeps detailed notes on all the weddings held at the Grand Palms. Unfortunately, his files are password protected.

"I already tried."

I also already tried googling the names of the guests who stayed in all of the rooms we cleaned that day, but as luck would have it, they all had super-common names—Jones and Brown and Garcia. So my internet sleuthing didn't turn up anything.

"Did you try Facebook?" Nalani says.

I pick my head up off the desk and look at her. "No."

She shrugs. "If I got married in Hawaii, I'd post millions of pictures."

I log in to Facebook and, one by one, I search through the names. But by the time I get to Ashley Rodriquez, I've started to give up hope again. How can there be so many people out there with the same name?

But then I spot a profile photo of a girl wearing a veil.

I sit up a little straighter. I click on this Ashley Rodriquez and, fortunately, her page isn't private. A rush of relief goes through me as I look through her feed and find pictures of her wedding—Ashley and her groom strolling on the beach, their backs to the camera, her veil trailing behind them. Standing so close, their noses are almost touching, her hands on the side of his face, her diamond wedding band catching the light. A close-up of their feet, *Just Maui'd* written in the sand. And one of the two of them posing in front of the chapel at the Grand Palms.

I smile. "You were right," I say to Nalani. "I found her!"

Nalani isn't cheering, like I expected her to. I glance up and find Will standing beside her, his hair in its messy Elvis pompadour, his hands stuffed into the front pocket of his black hoodie. Those dark rings under his eyes are back.

"Hey," I say. The smile slips from my face as I remember that I'm mad at him.

Nalani looks back and forth between us. "I should get running," she says. She takes off before I can stop her.

And before I can ask Will why he hasn't bothered texting me back, he says, "So. I talked to my dad. It did not go well." He lets out a breath and rubs the bridge of his nose. "I mean, I knew he wouldn't be thrilled that I don't want to go to Wharton, but he really freaked out."

"Maybe he'll come around," I say.

But Will's already shaking his head. "He won't. You don't know my dad," he says. "He never changes his mind. I'm going to business school, and then I'm working for him, and that's it. That's my life. All planned out."

"What about what you want?"

What about California? What about camping in the Redwood Forest? Staying in hostels, backpacking around the country, stargazing?

He snorts. "What I want isn't important."

"It is, though," I say. "It's your life."

"Marty, if I don't go along with this, then he'll cut me off."

"You think he'd really do that?" My mom can be a nightmare, but I can't imagine her disowning me.

"Oh, he'd do it," he says. "No question."

"Okay. Well, maybe that wouldn't be such a bad thing."

He looks at me like I've just spoken to him in Klingon. "It's the worst thing. I have no way of supporting myself."

"What about opening a coffee shop?"

"I need money for that." He grimaces. "It was a stupid idea, anyway. What do I know about running a coffee shop?"

"Well, maybe nothing now, but you could learn." I'm trying to help him, but it's pretty clear he doesn't want my help.

"It's never going to happen. It's just a dumb dream," he says.

But it's not dumb. Seeing him so defeated is the worst. I can't believe he's giving up so easily, just going to follow the path that his father has determined is the best one for him. I know what it's like to be afraid, to be so paralyzed by fear that you can't see clearly. But I also know that if he does give into it, he'll be miserable.

"With everything that's happened . . . I can't keep disappointing him," he says. "So I'm going to Wharton. That's it."

"It doesn't have to be."

He shakes his head. "I'm not like you, Marty. People

are counting on me. I have responsibilities. You don't understand."

I stiffen. He doesn't think I understand responsibility? I'm standing in front of him, working the graveyard shift, making sure rich tourists like him have an unforgettable vacation. Will Foster has never had to work a day in his life. I may not understand exactly what his life is like, but he doesn't understand mine, either.

"That came out wrong," he says, running a hand through his hair. "I'm sorry. I just . . . I was really hoping this would all work out."

I feel myself go cold all over. By "this," he must mean me.

It seems like he's made up his mind about his future and, by extension, about us. I let myself believe that we could be more than just a summer romance. All it took was his father showing up and he's suddenly aware that we come from different worlds. And I don't belong in his.

This was always going to be how it ended. So why do I feel so blindsided?

"I'm not sure what you want me to say," I reply.

"I guess there's nothing to say."

Tears prick my eyes. I knew better than to get involved with a tourist. Especially this summer, when my luck has been so awful. And it's about to get worse, because now I'm going to see Will around the hotel. I'll have to smile and pretend that everything's okay, that we never meant anything to each other.

As if he knows what I'm thinking, Will says, "I'm leaving tomorrow."

"What?"

"My parents found out that Hayes has been drinking again," he says. "They're sending us to stay with our grandmother in the Hamptons for the rest of the summer."

We stare at each other. There's really nothing else to say—nothing that will make this hurt any less, anyway.

This is for the best, I tell myself. Will and I aren't destined to be together. No amount of four-leaf clovers or wishing on stars can change that.

Will swallows. "I didn't mean for—"

"It's fine," I cut him off. "Really."

But it's so far from fine. And I'm not fooling him.

I pick up the stapler and start to fiddle with it. Will stands there for a minute, drumming his fingers on the counter, until the awful awkwardness gets to him and he leaves.

And somehow I manage to hold it together until he's disappeared.

Twenty-two

I sent the luggage tag back to Ashley Rodriquez this morning. As soon as I dropped it into the mailbox, my phone rang. It was Marielle, calling to tell me that the hotel's insurance would cover the cost of replacing my car. The amount is more than I ever expected, more than enough to buy a decent used car as well as fund a trip to California.

So I think Karma and I might be good.

But while I'm happy that my luck seems to be restored, I'm still feeling pretty crummy about what happened with Will last night. I hate how we left things. By now he's probably on a plane back to the East Coast, already tucking this trip—and me—away in his memory. I keep telling myself it's for the best, but it sure doesn't feel that way.

I'm sitting at a stoplight, thinking about Will, when I get a text from my brother. He wants me to meet him and my dad at Napili Bay. I haven't seen Ansel since he sprung my dad on me at Leoda's the other day. They're staying at a hotel in Kihei while my dad's in town, however long that will be.

I debate which direction to turn. Left will take me home. Right will take me to my dad.

The light turns green. I'm still not sure which way to turn, but the car behind me honks, and I find myself heading toward the beach.

Maybe it's time to stop running away. Maybe it's finally time to just deal.

———

I squeeze in behind Ansel's van on the narrow road. The sky is streaked with pink and gold as I walk through the grounds of the fancy restaurant perched on the bluff. I spot my brother right away, sitting on the beach. My dad is a short distance from him, standing alone on the rocks, watching the turtles fight their way to shore. Something about seeing him there, alone, makes me sad. Maybe it's because all the other times, I was standing right there beside him.

I kick my slippers off and walk across the warm sand toward my brother. Ansel gives me a tentative smile as I approach him.

"I didn't think you'd come," he says.

"I wasn't sure I would."

My brother holds out his hand and I help him stand up. He brushes the sand off his butt and then throws an arm around my shoulders. He smells like the ocean—he always smells like the ocean—and it's comforting to know that's one thing that will probably never change.

"So why aren't you over there with him?" I ask.

Ansel shrugs. "I just needed a minute to myself. He's driving me a bit crazy, to be honest. I'm starting to remember what it was like when he lived at home."

I snort. It wasn't easy. But then, having him leave wasn't easy, either.

"I'm sorry for dropping him on you like that the other day," Ansel says. "It was a pretty crappy thing for me to do."

"Very crappy."

He smiles. "You did just hear me apologize, right?"

I smile back. "I guess there's a first time for everything."

The sun dips lower in the sky. Two turtles have climbed onto the rock near my dad. He's crouched down and I know he's talking to them. I know this because he does it, every time.

"I gave Libby to Mrs. B.," I say.

My brother squeezes my shoulder. "See? Sometimes life works out."

Or sometimes it takes you in a direction you never expected. Like with me. I started this summer so sure that I was going to stay on Maui. But I finally realized that life is going to change whether I want it to or not. It won't make a difference if I stay in the same place, because this will no longer be the same place.

I also realized that staying with my mom is an excuse. She doesn't need me to help her heal. That's something she needs to do on her own.

"I'm going to California with Nalani," I say.

Ansel hoots and holds up his hand so I can high-five him. I slap his palm.

"As someone wise once told me, I can't live my life for someone else."

"To be honest, I didn't think you had it in you," Ansel adds. "You're always so . . . good." He shudders.

If he only knew about all the things I stole. I'm not the angel he thinks I am.

Dad stands up. He turns around and looks in our direction, but the sun is behind him, so I can't see his face. My hands are suddenly clammy.

"He feels bad," Ansel says. "I know—it's not enough, but it's a start, right?" He nudges me. "Where is staying angry with him going to get you?"

Probably nowhere. And if I wasn't ready to let go of it, to try to forgive my dad, then I guess I would have chosen to turn left at that stoplight.

"We're still a family," Ansel says quietly. "We just look a little different now."

I sigh. The distance between us isn't far now, but it still feels like a million miles. I guess it all starts with one step.

My brother stays put while I walk over and join my dad. When I get to where he is, he holds out his hand so I don't slip on the rocks. I let him help me up, but as soon as I'm beside him, I pull my hand away. I'm not quite ready to hug it out yet.

Dad clears his throat. "Ansel didn't tell me you were meeting us here."

I shrug. We silently watch another turtle climb onto the rocks and search for something to say to each other.

Not going to lie: this is awkward. We've lost the easy rhythm we once had. Right now I feel like I'm standing beside a stranger. I wipe my palms on my shorts. I have a thousand questions I'd like to ask him, beginning with why he left, but that's probably not the best way to start building a bridge between us.

Maybe what we need is an icebreaker.

"Would you rather win a gold medal or an academy award?" I ask him.

He gives me a puzzled look. "What?"

"A gold medal or academy award? Which would you rather have?"

It's a silly question, and I'm pretty sure I know how he's going to answer before he opens his mouth, but that's not the point. The point is that we need to get to know each other again. And as I've learned, playing this game is as good as any other way.

"Uh . . . gold medal, I guess," he says. "I was always pretty good at track."

I relax slightly. I'm relieved that he answered the way I expected he would. It gives me hope that we can get back to where we were, sooner rather than later.

"Your turn," I say.

"My turn to what?"

"Ask me a question."

"Okay." He thinks for a minute. "Would you rather eat tacos or ice cream?"

I roll my eyes. "You're not very good at this game."

He laughs and the sound goes right to my heart. It's been so long since I've heard him laugh—much longer than six months.

"Tacos," I say. "Always."

"I knew you'd say that."

The wind picks up. A wave crashes over the rocks, soaking our feet. The sun has almost totally disappeared now. My dad's face is lost in the shadows.

"We should probably go back," he says.

If only we could go back, I think as he holds out his hand again. I think about how we'll have to find a new way forward as we climb back down to the beach. This time, I let him hold my hand for a minute before I pull away.

"So how long are you in town for?" I ask as we walk back toward Ansel.

"As long as it takes for you to forgive me," Dad says. "Or till next Wednesday. Whichever comes first."

I frown. Getting our relationship back on track will take more than a few days. I wish I hadn't wasted all this time avoiding him.

"I would like to stay longer, but unfortunately I have to get back to work," he adds.

Work. I know nothing about his life on O'ahu. This is what Ansel's been trying to tell me—I've never given my dad a chance to explain. All those times he called, I just let him go to voice mail. I shut him out.

"I'm sorry it took me so long to get here," he says. "I'm sorry about a lot of things. But I'm going to keep coming back here until you've forgiven me."

For the first time, I realize my dad doesn't have all the answers. He's not perfect; he's made mistakes. And I certainly haven't always done what's right—stealing from hotel guests proved that. I can continue to lock him out, or I can take a chance and let him back in.

"I'd like that," I say.

He smiles at me and draws me into a hug and we stand there, watching the sea turtles, until the last bit of sun has disappeared.

Twenty-three

The next morning I'm sitting on my bed, searching for flights to California on my laptop and trying not to think about Will, when my mom comes down to my room. I don't look at her when she enters. I'm still mad that she sent Libby to the shelter, but I'm also feeling super guilty—both because I'm leaving the island and because I'm meeting my dad and Ansel for breakfast shortly. I don't want her to feel like she's alone or that I'm abandoning her.

"I hear you're back on nights," she says, handing me a mug of hibiscus tea.

News travels fast. Marielle must have filled her in.

"Yeah. I have a shift tonight."

I haven't quit the hotel yet, but I'm going to give my

notice in the next few days. This would be a good time to tell my mom my plans, but until everything is official, I want to keep this to myself.

I take a sip of tea as she walks over to my desk. She starts to straighten my books, arranging them into a tidy pile, spines lined up. I watch her roll a pair of Alice in Wonderland knee socks into a ball and walk over to stuff them in my dresser.

"Did you come down here just to clean my room?" I ask her.

She sighs and closes my dresser drawer. "No," she says. "I came down here to apologize." She comes over and sits at the end of my bed. "I'm sorry about the cat. I shouldn't have taken it to the shelter without talking to you first."

I know I was wrong to bring Libby back here—and to keep her for so long—but it's nice to know that my mom feels bad, too.

"I was angry that you deliberately ignored me and brought her here," she continues. "Once I calmed down, I went back to the shelter, but—"

"Wait. You went back to get her?"

"I'm not heartless, Marty," she says. "And I hadn't changed my mind about keeping her—I don't want a cat—but I thought that maybe I'd overreacted and we could look after her until you found her a home. By the time I went back, someone had already adopted her."

"I went back," I say. "I didn't adopt her, but I did find a home for her." I tell her about giving Libby to Mrs. B.

"Well, I'm glad it all worked out." She gives me a hug. She stands up to leave, but at the door, she turns and looks back at me.

"Everything else okay?"

I nod. I'm mostly excited for what's ahead and where the future will take me, but I'm still nervous about all the change coming my way. I'm also sad about Will. It sucks that it didn't work out between us. But I don't want to focus on what might have been, so instead I'm going to remember his smile and the way he looked at me. I'll remember this summer and how he made me feel.

"I will be," I say.

———

When Benjie comes back from his break the next night, he gives me this strange, self-satisfied smile, like he has some big secret or something.

I narrow my eyes at him. "What?"

His smile widens. He mimes like he's locking his lips, then tosses away the imaginary key.

"Why are you being weird?"

"Nothing weird about me," he says.

"Okay then." The best way to get information out of Benjie is to pretend I don't care, so I go back to texting Nalani about our trip. She's trying to talk me into renting a camper van instead of staying in hostels, but I'm not sold on the idea. Spending one night in the hotel van in Hana was rough enough—I can't imagine living in one for four months.

All of a sudden, I feel Benjie behind me. He starts to fuss with my ponytail.

I swat at him. "What are you doing?"

"I'm bored," he says. "Let me do your hair."

"No."

"Come on," he wheedles. "It'll be fun!"

"Fun for who?"

"For me."

I sigh, knowing he'll just pester me until I give in. I pull out the elastic holding my hair back. Benjie produces a brush from somewhere and starts to comb my hair, more gently than I ever would have guessed that he could be.

My phone beeps. Nalani's sent me a photo of a van painted in an eye-wateringly bright psychedelic rainbow, like something straight out of the flower-child sixties.

It has a kitchen!

No, I text back.

Benjie starts to braid the side of my hair, carefully avoiding the bandage on my forehead. Marielle wasn't happy when I showed up for work like this, but I need money now more than ever, so there was no way I was calling in sick.

When Benjie finishes, he gathers the braid into a ponytail and then secures it with my elastic. He takes my phone out of my hands and snaps a picture, then turns the phone around so I can admire his handiwork.

"Voilà!"

"Nice," I say.

"Nice?" He snorts. "It's fabulous." He tucks a flyaway strand of hair that somehow didn't make it into the ponytail behind my ear. His lower lip begins to tremble. "I'm really going to miss you." He's been sensitive all night, ever since I told him that I'm planning to quit the hotel.

"Are you crying?"

"No." He swipes at his eyes.

I give him a hug. "I'm going to miss you, too."

"Who am I going to play Hangman with?"

I laugh.

He goes over to his computer and starts checking out gossip sites, but I feel him sneaking glances at me every few minutes.

"What?"

"Nothing," he says. "You just look really pretty."

I blink. What is going on with him?

The desk phone rings. I make a move to answer it, but he beats me to it—which is super strange because Benjie never wants to answer the phone. At this time of night, it's either someone calling from overseas to make a reservation or a guest calling to complain about something—and neither of those are things he likes to deal with.

"Front desk," Benjie says. "Uh-huh. Uh-huh. Okay. Yes, of course, right away."

He sets the phone down and says, "Something's going on in the ballroom. Would you mind going over there and checking it out?"

"No way." It's almost midnight and the ballroom is all the way on the other side of the hotel. "Send security."

Benjie sighs and rubs his forehead. "I'm the worst at this." He walks over to me and rests his hands on my shoulders and stares deeply into my eyes. "You need to go to the ballroom."

"Why?"

He smiles and straightens the collar on my uniform. "Just trust me. What's waiting for you there is not something you want to miss."

What could be waiting for me in the ballroom?

I stiffen. Or . . . maybe it's not a what. Maybe it's a who.

"Go," Benjie says. "And don't worry about rushing back. I've got it covered."

My hands are shaking as I walk through the lobby and down the deserted hall that leads to the east wing. It takes me five minutes to get to the ballroom, but it feels much longer. It feels like the longest walk of my life.

I tell myself not to get my hopes up. Will left two days ago. Whatever this surprise is, it can't be him.

But I can't help it: my hopes are up. Way, way up.

When I finally arrive at the ballroom, the doors are closed. I stand in front of them for a minute, trying to steady my breath. I'm afraid to open the doors and find out that Will isn't on the other side. I'm afraid of having my heart crushed again.

But I guess there's only one way to find out.

I take a deep breath and pull open one of the doors.

My eyes widen. The ballroom has been transformed into a winter wonderland. I walk under a white balloon arch into the all-white room. It's like being inside a snow globe. Fairy lights are strung everywhere, hanging from the ceiling and twinkling in the branches of banyan trees. There's a table with a full luau feast, in the center of which is an ice sculpture of my high school, Maui High.

I shake my head. This is my prom. Somehow, unbelievably, this is my prom.

And even more unbelievably, there, in the middle of the dance floor, is Will. Wearing a black tux with red Converse sneakers, his dark hair combed neatly back. A white plumeria flower is pinned to his lapel. He's holding a matching corsage in his hand.

He gives me a nervous smile as I meet him underneath the glittering disco ball.

"How . . . ?" I say.

He slips the corsage onto my wrist, the pink-tipped flowers soft against my skin. "I had a little help."

I smile. Nalani. She was on the prom committee.

"I can't believe you did this." My hands are shaking as I reach over and straighten his bow tie, which is the exact shade of blue of the dress I wore to prom. I wish I was in that dress now instead of my ugly uniform, but Will doesn't seem to notice. I send a silent thank-you to Benjie for fixing my hair.

"I thought you could use a do-over," Will says.

This is so much better than my original prom. And

not just because chances are high that I won't catch Will making out with Grace Hamasaki. It's because I'm with him.

"Wait," I say. "What are you doing here? I thought you'd already gone back to the mainland?"

He shrugs. "I convinced my dad to give me an extra few days. I had something important to take care of first."

The fact that he stayed—that he did all of this for me—makes my heart swell. I smile and move a little closer to him, until there's no distance left between us.

"You must be a good negotiator," I say.

"Not good enough to change his mind about business school," he replies. "But I'm learning."

The opening strains of "Africa" start to play. I laugh as Will slides his arms around my waist. I put my arms around his neck, my fingers winding through the back of his hair, wanting this moment to last forever. We move slowly around the dance floor, the disco ball casting stars of light on us.

"I wish . . . ," he murmurs. There's so much feeling behind those two words that he doesn't even need to finish the sentence. I know exactly what he's wishing for.

"Me too." I rest my head on his shoulder and close my eyes.

Maybe this is our last dance. Or maybe, if we're really lucky, we'll cross paths again someday. I can't predict the future, but I'd like to believe this isn't where our story ends. I'd like to believe that this isn't just a summer romance and that the universe will find a way to bring us back together.

But I'll think about that tomorrow. In the meantime, we have this one night. This one perfect night.

And for now, that's enough.

Acknowledgments

It really does take a village to get a book on the shelves. Lucky for me, my village includes the amazingly talented people at Swoon Reads, as well as Hannah Fergesen, KT Literary, one heck of a great literary agent.

Thank you to my insightful and thoughtful editor, Kat Brzozowski. Thank you, Jean Feiwel, Lauren Scobell, Emily Settle, Morgan Rath, Mandy Veloso, Kaitlin Severini, and Becca Syracuse, who designed the perfect cover for this book. Thank you, as well, to Fernanda Viveiros at Raincoast Books and to the many bloggers, librarians, booksellers, and readers who have supported me and my books over the past few years.

One of the many benefits of being published with

Swoon Reads is being part of a very supportive, generous circle of writers. I'm grateful for all of you. Extra thanks to Sandy Hall and Tiana Smith for the feedback on this book in its earliest, messiest stages.

Thank you, Jarren MacDougall-McLean, for lifting the curtain on what it's like to work in a hotel, and Prerna Pickett and Nikki Van De Car, for reading through the manuscript with a keen eye.

Thank you to my friends and family: Mike and Tila Cassone, Chris and Carla Cassone, Ray Dosanj and Harpreet Gill, Leiko Greaves, Abby Wener Herlin, Brian and Joy Honeybourn, Barbara Hsiao, Kate Hunter, Mandy James, James and Elizabeth Koprich, Tracey Lundell, Shaun and Carianne McKay, Jennifer McKenzie, Pam Morrison, Stacie Palivos, Karam and Varinder Rai, Nadine Silver, Jim and Jela Stanic, Robert Stanic and Ange Grim, and Anna Tennick.

And, as always, thank you to my husband, Tony, for his unwavering love and support—and for agreeing to move all the way across the country so I could continue to follow my dreams. And to our daughter, Lila, my lucky charm.